Deadly Kin

Tom Eslick *DEADLY KIN*

Viking

VIKING
Published by the Penguin Group
Penguin Group (USA) Inc., 375 Hudson Street, New York, NY 10014, U.S.A.
Penguin Books Ltd, 80 Strand, London WC2R 0RL, England
Penguin Books Australia Ltd, 250 Camberwell Road, Camberwell,
    Victoria 3124, Australia
Penguin Books Canada Ltd, 10 Alcorn Avenue,
    Toronto, Ontario, Canada M4V 3B2
Penguin Books India (P) Ltd, 11 Community Centre, Panchsheel Park,
    New Delhi – 110 017, India
Penguin Books (N.Z.) Ltd, Cnr Rosedale and Airborne Roads, Albany,
    Auckland, New Zealand
Penguin Books (South Africa) (Pty) Ltd, 24 Sturdee Avenue,
    Rosebank, Johannesburg 2196, South Africa

Penguin Books Ltd, Registered Offices:
80 Strand, London WC2R 0RL, England

First published in 2003 by Viking Penguin,
a member of Penguin Group (USA) Inc.

10   9   8   7   6   5   4   3   2   1

PUBLISHER'S NOTE
This is a work of fiction. Names, characters, places, and incidents either are the product of the author's imagination or are used fictitiously, and any resemblance to actual persons, living or dead, business establishments, events, or locales is entirely coincidental.

LIBRARY OF CONGRESS CATALOGING IN PUBLICATION DATA
Eslick, Tom.
    Deadly kin : a White Mountains mystery / Tom Eslick.
        p.   cm.
    ISBN 0-670-03248-4
    1. New Hampshire—Fiction   I. Title.
PS3605.S755D43   2003
813'.6—dc21   2003043089

This book is printed on acid-free paper. ∞

Printed in the United States of America
Set in Bembo, with Aperto display
Designed by Carla Bolte

FOR SUSAN, MY WIFE

ACKNOWLEDGMENTS I would like to thank lawyers John B. Pendleton and John T. Pendleton, father and son, for their invaluable advice about New Hampshire law; Gail Paine for allowing me to visit the Carroll County House of Corrections; my good friend and colleague David Pilla for letting me borrow his class presentation on the life cycle of the meningeal worm; my agent Alison J. Picard for her efforts in placing this novel; and my editor Susan Hans O'Connor for her expertise and belief in my work.

Deadly Kin

Chapter 1

THE TRAIL TO THE ZEALAND FALLS HUT WAS FLECKED
with early signs of fall color, the birches just beginning to
show yellow, the swamp maples, a deep blood maroon. The
afternoon light, slanted and brilliant, brought the woods into
sharp relief.

In an effort to break an icy silence, Will Buchanan said,
"See the way the sun hits the stream? Makes the water jump,
doesn't it."

Erin Wickham stopped and shielded her eyes against the
glare off the water. She hadn't said a word since they had
started up from the parking lot. Will wondered if the whole
trip was going to be like this.

She turned away from the water and eyed him curiously.
"When did you and my aunt break up anyway?" she said.

The question, unexpected and blunt, caught Will off
guard, and now it was his turn not to say anything. He fiddled
with the sternum strap on his backpack.

Erin pressed. "She said you two used to live together."

"That's right."

"What happened?"

Will wasn't about to talk to anybody about Laurie, but especially not to a teenager he didn't know well. "We'd better
get going," he said.

The trail was wide enough for them to walk shoulder to
shoulder. Will hated the idea that Laurie had talked to this kid
about their relationship. He was sorry now he had agreed to
lead Erin to the hut to meet up with her brother, who was
thru-hiking the Appalachian Trail.

As they came to a footbridge, Erin stopped. "I'm sorry, Mr. Buchanan," she said. "I was out of line."

"That's okay."

"I just don't like to see my aunt so unhappy."

She's unhappy? He almost said it out loud. "I guess Laurie and I have to work out a few things."

"Yeah. That's what she said."

"She told you that?"

Before Erin could answer, an elderly couple approached the footbridge from the other end. Even though the busy summer season was over, the trail to Zealand Falls remained a popular destination, an easy, flat day hike in.

"Afternoon," the man said. He pulled off his snap-brim hat and wiped his forehead with the back of his hand.

Will studied the hat. There was a hole right where the crease came together. It was a great hat, once elegant, now sweat stained. "You folks come from the hut?" he said.

"That's right." The old man raked the top of his head with his fingers. His white hair stood up like a rooster's cap.

The woman, diminutive, smiled attentively. "We stayed there last night," she said. "You headed that way?"

"We are."

The hut system in the White Mountain National Forest provides hikers with the amenities of a bunk room and a meal. It costs about as much as a decent motel room to stay overnight, but it feels like a real bargain and a luxury when you've been in the woods for a while.

"Well, we've got to keep moving," the old man said. He stuck his hat back on his head and ran his finger along the brim.

The old woman smiled as they passed Will and Erin. Her walking stick plunked on the bridge. "Say hi to Kevin for me," she said.

"Kevin?" Will said.

"The hutsman."

Erin said after they left, "They seem like nice people."

"Hikers usually are."

"So this hut is really a fancy place?"

"I wouldn't call it 'fancy.' Comfortable, maybe."

"It will be great to see Josh again."

"How long's your brother been on the trail?"

"Since April."

They started walking again. The encounter with the elderly couple seemed to have dispelled the awkwardness Will had felt with Erin, and she grew more voluble with her increasing excitement over seeing her brother.

"He's been hiking the trail in honor of Jacko," she said. "Did Aunt Laurie tell you that?"

"Who's Jacko?"

"Oh, I'm sorry. I forgot you weren't family. You and my aunt have been so close. . . ."

Will wondered if she really did forget he wasn't family and her comment was just another attempt to pry into his life. "So who is he?"

"Jackson Lloyd. My mother married him after she divorced my father. When he was a little boy, Josh couldn't pronounce his name and called him Jacko. It stuck, and the whole family started to call him that."

"And Jacko died?"

"Yes."

"Aunt Laurie didn't tell me anything about that."

Erin stopped. She pulled on Will's arm and held on to his sleeve. "What did she tell you about me?"

"Nothing. She just said she had to be on duty and couldn't take you in to meet Josh and would I be so kind as to do it." Will had been used to doing favors for Laurie. As a small-town chief of police, she had little time off.

Erin let her hand drop. "You really don't know anything about me, then, do you?"

"Only that you're Laurie's niece. That you're new to the school."

"I appreciate you doing this."

"Yeah, sure. No problem."

"You still like my aunt, don't you."

Will stared at her for a moment, then turned up the trail again.

Erin caught up to him. "Okay, so I won't mention it again."

"I'd appreciate it."

"I know why you're doing this, though."

Will stopped. "Look. Your aunt Laurie asked me to help. I said yes."

"Points."

"What?"

"You're doing this to get points with her."

"I'm doing this because she asked me to," Will repeated. "I'm doing her a favor."

"Nobody does something for nothing," Erin said.

———

Will and Erin climbed up on to the porch of the Zealand Falls Hut and found Kevin beating the dust out of a floor mat with a stubby broom.

Kevin sported a full but stringy beard. He grunted as he swatted the mat. The sound of their boots on the porch startled him, and he whirled around. "Guess I didn't hear you coming."

"Sorry," Will said.

Kevin's face was red from his efforts. "You must be the two I've been expecting." Equipped with a two-way radio, each hut has a reservation system linked together and with the headquarters in Pinkham Notch. Laurie had called in to make sure there was still room left and had reserved a spot for them.

Will dropped his pack on the porch, and Kevin led them into the front room of the hut. He wore hiking boots and shorts that, because of his stumpy legs, draped over his knees. The one-floor log building was the size of a double-wide mobile home, and the front room served as kitchen/dining room as well as souvenir shop. A bunk room on each side, one each for male and female, completed the layout.

Kevin checked his clipboard. "So you're Josh and Erin."

"Not quite," Will said. "This is Erin. Josh is on his way."

Kevin looked puzzled. He pushed his ball cap back. His head was shaved bald. "I guess I don't have you down."

"I'll be staying outside," Will said. "The reservation's for brother and sister. He's coming in off the AT."

"Gotcha."

"Any good places to camp nearby?"

Kevin didn't look up but pointed his pencil to the southwest. "Anywhere upstream." He put the clipboard down on the glass case that housed souvenir T-shirts and ball caps, maps, candy bars, and compasses.

"You must be closing for the season soon," Will said.

"Two weeks. The twenty-third, officially."

"So this hut doesn't stay open for the winter?"

"Well, sort of. It's self-service, with a caretaker."

Erin suddenly cut in. "I'll be out on the porch," she said.

Kevin's head snapped back. He had apparently been so busy with his clipboard that he hadn't gotten a good look at her. "Yeah, I guess all this talk's kinda boring." He stumbled over his words.

Erin nodded, turned, and headed toward the porch. Kevin's eyes didn't leave her, and it took a while after the screen door slammed for him to turn them back to Will.

Will grinned at him, and Kevin colored. "So," Will said, "people snowshoe in here in the winter?"

"What? Oh, yeah. Or ski."

"Get many thru-hikers?" The term was reserved for those attempting to hike the entire length of the AT.

"Sometimes. Only two can stay the night, though."

"I guess you have to limit the number."

"We let them work for their keep. Don't charge them anything." Kevin was still looking over Will's shoulder at Erin on the porch.

"She's seventeen," Will said.

"She is?"

"A student at Saxton Mills."

"A boarding school, right?"

Will nodded. "Just down the road." He pulled out his wallet. "How much for the two of them?"

"Oh, yeah. Guess I'm not being too professional, here." Kevin flipped over a well-used, laminated price chart and ran his finger down one of the columns. "One-twenty. Includes dinner and breakfast tomorrow."

Will peeled off six twenties.

"You sure you don't want to stay? I just baked a carrot cake."

Will shook his head. "I sleep better in a tent."

Will pushed open the screen door and found that Erin had left the porch. He leaned over the railing and scouted her out down on the ledge where the falls drop a good fifty feet. The hut was nestled in close to the edge of the water—a healthy, rushing stream, no more—which cut through a series of ledges, leaving exposed rock on either side.

Erin was sunning herself on the rocks, her legs stretched out, back arched, face raised to the October light. It reminded Will of poses that forties starlets assumed in grainy black-and-white photos. The light was catching her short-cropped auburn hair, giving the impression that it was dancing with fire. Yes, Kevin. She is only seventeen. Maybe seventeen going on thirty. Will couldn't put his finger on it, but something about her, besides her obvious beauty, spelled trouble. He remembered what Erin had said earlier that afternoon about not really knowing who she was, and he guessed that Laurie had not told him everything about her niece.

Will walked down the steps of the porch and strode out onto the rocks. He passed a sign that read CAUTION: LEDGE IS STEEP AND SLIPPERY.

He whistled a nondescript tune so that his approach wouldn't startle her, but apparently the sound of the water drowned him out. She jerked sharply when his shadow fell over her.

"Sorry. I tried to let you know I was coming." Will sat next to her, and she assumed her glamour-girl pose again.

"This is cool," she said. "I could sit here for hours."

"It is pleasant."

"If I had come here on SMOOT, I would have been a happier camper."

"Where did you end up?"

"God knows."

"Well, who were you with?"

"Mrs. Lawerizack and Ms. Campbell."

Will thought a moment. "Then you were in the Pemi."

"The what?"

"The Pemigewasset Wilderness."

Erin sighed. "Whatever."

SMOOT stands for the Saxton Mills Outdoor Orientation Trip, five days of backpacking in the Whites, run at the beginning of each school year for all incoming students. He imagined that the trip with Lawerizack and Campbell had challenged Erin's hiking abilities as well as the leaders' patience. Today's hike had been a short one, but Will already surmised that Erin was not in her element.

"Have any idea when your brother's supposed to be passing through?"

"His letter said in the afternoon." The mention of her brother brought her upright to a sitting position. She hugged her knees. "I miss him so much."

"When was the last time you saw him?"

"Not since he left last April. I could have met him in Hanover, but I had to do the stupid SMOOT thing."

"You say he's doing this trip in honor of his father. Mind telling me how Jacko died?"

She looked out over the falls. "They say he drowned."

She didn't add to that, and Will let her words sit a moment.

"It's been really hard on Josh," she said.

"How old is he?"

"Just turned twenty."

"He drop out of school?"

"Never went to college. There was a big argument with Jacko about it. Then Jacko drowned, and Josh is, like, you know, carrying this big sack of guilt now."

Will tried to imagine what a sack of guilt looked like. "They never patched things up?"

Erin shook her head no. "And to make it worse, Josh inherits a big chunk of his estate when he's twenty-one."

This is a burden? When Will's grandfather died, he left him a set of woodworking tools and the balance of a thirty-year mortgage to pay off. Will didn't mind. He felt he was giving back to a man who'd raised him after his own parents had passed away. He also got land and a hunting camp in Quebec, something he didn't mind paying for.

Will listened to the rushing water. He wanted to ask more questions, but he knew that it was better to mind his own business.

"If they could just find him," Erin said. She let her head rest on her arms.

"What?"

"Oh. Sorry. I guess I was thinking out loud."

"Find who?"

"Jacko. They never found his body."

———

By the time Will and Erin made it back to the hut, another hiker had arrived. Will glanced at the backpack leaning against the porch, a brand-new Kelty. The hiker, a stout woman Will guessed to be in her mid-fifties, sat on the porch steps, preoccupied with taking off her boot.

"I'm going to kill him," she said to no one in particular. With a theatrical grimace, she gave the boot a final yank.

"Kill who?" Will said.

She looked up. "The damn salesman who sold me these things." She began to work on the other boot. Her accent was guttural—German or Austrian.

Will picked up the discarded boot and stuck his hand inside. "Looks like it could stand some breaking in," he said.

"Tell me about it," she said.

"Your toes hitting the end?"

She thrust her foot forward. "Feast your eyes," she said. The sock was bloodied at the toes.

Will knelt down. "Let's have a look," he said.

"No. Don't touch it." She pulled her leg back abruptly, and her foot accidentally hit Will's hand as he reached to examine it.

"Ouch. Damn you."

"He's only trying to help," Erin said.

"Mind your own business, young lady."

"Okay. Let's all just calm down," Will said.

"It's my business if you're being rude to a friend," Erin said.

"I said that's enough." Will stood up and put his hands on Erin's shoulders. She tensed. He let his hands drop and said calmly, "Why don't you stand down there at the head of the trail and watch for Josh."

Erin hooked her thumbs in the belt loops of her jeans and smiled at Will. "Whatever," she said. As she turned to leave, her eyes met the woman's dead-on.

The woman shouted at her back as she descended the stairs, "You are an impudent young woman!"

The voices brought Kevin to the porch. "Everything okay out here?"

"Everything's fine," Will said.

"Is that little brat staying here tonight?" the woman said.

"This is all my fault, Kevin," Will said. "I should have asked this woman first if she wanted my help."

Will's arguable admission of guilt had the effect of letting the air out of the woman. "No. It's my fault." Tears welled up. "I don't know why I came. I thought I'd never get here."

Kevin looked first to the woman, then back to Will. "I don't want any trouble."

"You have a med kit, Kevin?" Will said. "She's got some really sore toes."

"Sure thing."

Will watched the woman as she choked back sobs. He felt like putting his hand on her shoulder, but he didn't want to get bit again. "I understand it must have been tough walking," he said. "You can doctor the toes yourself if you want. I won't touch them. You just need to take care of them."

Kevin came out with the med kit and handed it to Will, who opened it for the woman and held it out to her.

The woman looked at it like she didn't know what it was. She started shivering.

"You feel cold, ma'am?" Will said.

"No. I'm okay."

It hit Will suddenly that her ill temper might be due to factors other than mere personality. She was probably hypothermic. "What's your name, ma'am?"

"Helga."

"Helga Holt?" Kevin asked.

"Yes."

"You're on my list," Kevin said.

"Let's get you inside, Helga," Will said. "It's warmer in there."

He and Kevin helped Helga up, and she leaned on Will as he led her into the hut. Kevin gathered the med kit and followed. As Will walked her inside, he admonished himself for not using his head. One of the early signs of hypothermia is crankiness, and he should have suspected that Helga was tired and exhausted, that the feet weren't the real problem, long before the argument on the porch broke out. At times he wondered if he was beginning to lose what he had always trusted most: his instincts, his woods savvy.

"Got a blanket, Kevin?" Will asked, helping Helga to a chair.

"I'm really tired," Helga said. "I want to lie down."

"Let's get some tea in you first," Will said. "You'll feel better."

"The water's on," Kevin said.

"Your blood sugar might be a little low, too," Will said. "How about a candy bar?"

"I guess so. I'm not very hungry, though."

"Believe me. You'll feel better with something in your stomach."

"If you think so."

"You have a jacket? Another layer?" Will said.

Helga nodded. "In my pack."

Will headed back outside to retrieve the jacket. Before he reached the porch, he heard Erin yelp, "Oh, my God! You're here!"

He pushed open the screen door in time to see her embracing someone who could only be her brother Josh, who had just thrown his pack down and lifted her off the ground. It was the deep kiss that froze Will in his tracks. He'd seen sisterly kisses before, and this was *not* one of them.

Chapter 2

THE KISS LASTED LONG ENOUGH FOR WILL TO FIGHT the urge to break it up. If he'd a bucket of water, he'd have dumped it on them. He made a lot of noise clumping down the porch stairs. "So you're Josh," he said.

Josh didn't end the embrace first. It was Erin who remembered herself and gently pushed Josh away.

Her cheeks were flushed. "This is Mr. Buchanan, Josh," she said. She straightened her blouse. "He was kind enough to be my guide."

Will shook hands with Josh. His grip was strong, the tendons in his arm springing to life as Will squeezed. Josh traveled light—T-shirt, shorts, and hiking boots—with probably just socks, polypro, pack stove, and pasta in his trim pack.

"I appreciate your being her chaperon, sir," Josh said.

Will hated the prissy-sounding "chaperon," but in this case, if that's the way Josh saw him, it was all to the good. "Glad to do it," he said.

Josh stood tall, a few inches above Will's six feet. Despite having been on the trail for a while, Josh was clean-shaven, his dark hair recently combed, and he smelled of cologne.

Erin squeezed Josh around the middle. "God, I've missed you," she said.

Will felt again that he should, like some boxing referee, break up the clinches. Instead he walked around them. "Excuse me," he said. "I need to get at Helga's pack."

"How is the witch?" Erin said.

Will turned and looked at her. "That's enough, Erin."

Erin didn't respond. She seemed suprised at the stern tone

in Will's voice. She held his eyes for a moment, then looked at the ground.

Josh grinned. "Hey, what's going on?"

Will opened Helga's pack and found a patterned fleece jacket. "I'm sure Erin will tell you all about it."

He headed back into the hut and found Helga still sitting up, drinking tea. Kevin was regaling her with some story. She seemed in better spirits.

"Put this on," Will said. "It'll get your blood flowing." He handed her the fleece.

"Thank you," she said. "I guess I really have been rude."

"Don't think anything about it," Will said.

"I don't usually pick fights."

The screen door opened, and two men entered. They were both about Josh's height, dressed in army fatigues.

"Ah. The last ones on my list," Kevin said. He left his spot at the table and approached them.

"How many does that make?" Helga asked.

Kevin put his pen in his shirt pocket. "Just five tonight. It'll pick up when the color peaks in a week or so."

Will turned to Helga. "Light's going fast," he said. "I need to find a place to camp before it gets dark."

"You're not staying here?" Helga looked genuinely disappointed.

"I don't sleep well with a bunch of people around." Will turned to leave.

"Wait a minute," Helga said. "What's your name?"

Will told her.

"If you have time," she said, "I *would* appreciate your looking at my feet."

A peace offering. "Sure," he said.

Will nodded to the two hikers dressed in fatigues as he passed them on his way out to the porch. He leaned over the railing. Erin and Josh had gone somewhere. He scanned the area, including the flat rocks near the falls, but there was no sign of them.

———

Will remembered Kevin's advice about staying toward the southwest to find a place to camp. He put on his pack and headed up the trail. To his left was a jury-rigged pump that supplied the hut with water.

Will had forgotten the beauty of the Zealand Falls area. He could remember only one other time he'd been at the hut, just passing through. It felt good to stretch his legs. He stopped every now and again to listen to the water rushing.

In all his years hiking the White Mountains, he had never stayed in a hut like the one at Zealand Falls. He felt that such places defeated the purpose of being in the woods. Why spend the night with a bunch of people you don't know when, usually, the main reason for going in is to get away from them?

The forest in the valley below was still illuminated, but up ahead a gray light washed the mountainside, the setting sun blocked by the ridge. He figured he had about a half hour of light left, just time enough to find a spot and pitch his small dome tent.

About fifty yards up from the hut, the terrain flattened, and he began to look to his right. He headed into the woods, dense with a grove of spruce at the edge of the trail. He looked up to find a birch stand farther in, and he trudged toward it. He knew, according to no-trace-camping etiquette, he should try to find a spot at least fifty yards in from the trail, well hidden from view. Given the fading light and terrain, this was not going to happen.

He stopped to examine an area that looked promising, when his attention was redirected by something moving to his left. In the half-light, he thought it might be a deer.

He crouched and peered through spaces in the scrub growth and discovered Erin and Josh.

They had thrown their clothes off and were lying on their sides in each other's arms. Josh was gently stroking Erin's thigh, and Erin had her hand on Josh's erection. She rolled over and guided him into her, and they came together violently.

Will turned away. He stared at the ground in shock. What kind of brother-sister act was this? Should he bust them or have a good talk with them later? A chaperon test if there ever was one.

He decided to pretend he hadn't seen them, pitch his tent with a great deal of fanfare, and hope they had sense enough to get the hell out of there—the chicken's way out, but it would have to do.

When he stood up to reach for his pack, he thought he detected other movement in the spruce grove near the trail. He strained his eyes but saw nothing. He turned back to the tent, and out of the corner of his eye he caught a glimpse of something disappearing into the darkness of the grove. It was just a brief instant, but Will couldn't shake the idea that the form was human.

He would have to check for tracks in the morning, but his gut told him that someone else had been there to watch the show.

———

It was only after Will had finished whistling a rendition of "Amazing Grace" and threaded the sleeves of the tent with the lightweight fiberglass poles that he checked on Erin and Josh; he was relieved to find they had managed to separate themselves and disappear.

But who else had been watching? The question preoccupied him as he completed pitching the tent. And should he stay in the hut to make sure the two remained uncoupled?

The more he thought about it, the less he considered it a good idea. He imagined himself lying awake listening for night sounds. The thought sickened him. He hadn't come all the way out here to be a vice cop. He would report to Laurie what he'd seen, but that would be it. The bunk rooms should keep them separate anyway. Let Kevin throw water on them.

Will decided, though, to put in an appearance at the hut before turning in. By the time he had made it to the trail again, it was dark. The sky was clear, with the stars just beginning to show. It would be a cold night. He tied a bandanna to a small poplar as a flag to alert him where to enter the woods on the way back. He flicked on his flashlight and headed down to the hut.

When he entered through the screen door, he was relieved to find that Erin and Josh had made it back. They sat huddled together on a couch in the corner holding hands. They looked up when he came in. Erin showed little sign that she might have known he'd seen them in action.

"There you two are," Will said.

Erin smiled at Josh. "We went for a walk." She hooked her arm through his. "I'm sorry. We should have told you."

It didn't sound genuine. "I wanted you to know where I

was camped," Will said. He told them about the bandanna tied to the tree. "I thought I'd turn in early."

Dinner wasn't quite ready. The rest of the ensemble were in attendance, waiting with an air of expectancy most likely inspired by the sweet smell of cornbread baking. The two young men dressed in fatigues were trading parts of a newspaper, and Helga was sitting on a stool talking to Kevin as he stirred a pot of chili.

Will got up to leave. "Well, good night everybody." He waved at the group.

Helga slipped off her stool and limped toward him. "You mean you're not even going to have dinner?"

"I've got food in my pack," he said.

"There's plenty," Kevin chimed in. He held the ladle in the air.

"Thanks, but I think I'll be heading back."

Helga said, "Before you go, let me introduce my two new friends." She gestured toward the guys in fatigues. "This is Marvin and Jared."

They were both lean and hard. Marvin was a tad shorter than Jared, faintly freckled with close-cropped red hair. Jared, olive skinned, had dark, penetrating eyes. Will shook hands.

"They're Marines, you know," Helga said.

The men were so quiet that Will wondered if Helga had become their spokesperson. He was pleased that she'd come around. She was certainly in a better mood than when he'd last seen her. Her cheeks had some color.

"And look," she said, lifting her foot. "They fixed me up real good."

Will checked the dressing. "Looks like you've been well taken care of," he said. "Before you take off tomorrow, you might want to paint your toes with tincture of benzoate. It'll toughen the skin."

Kevin said, "There's some in the med kit."

Will directed his eyes to the two men. "You guys from New Hampshire?"

"Jared is," Marvin said. "I'm from San Diego."

Will smiled. "You on a special detail?"

"Just a little R&R," Jared said. "Thought I'd show Marvin the Whites. He thinks New Hampshire's part of Vermont."

Marvin blushed. "It's not quite that bad," he said. There was a boyish innocence about him that seemed out of place in someone, Will knew, who was trained as a killing ma-chine—an odd package.

Will was pleased that these two were going to be in the hut. Their presence at least ensured an impression of law and order.

"Dinner's ready," Kevin said.

As the group took their places at the table, Will pulled Josh and Erin aside. He said to Erin, "How are you and Helga get-ting along?"

"We're ignoring each other."

"Give her the benefit of the doubt," Will said. "She was in real pain before."

Josh said, "I still don't know what happened."

Erin sighed. "It's nothing." She placed her hand on Will's arm. "I'm sorry about this, Mr. Buchanan. I'll try to be nice."

"See if you can mend some fences."

"I'll talk to her," she said.

Josh smiled. His teeth were remarkably even. "Don't you worry about a thing, Mr. Buchanan. We've got everything under control."

The night did not pass easily for Will. He kept thinking about Erin and Josh, the X-rated wood nymphs, and, despite himself, he was curious how long this relationship had been going on.

He couldn't shake the feeling that he'd been set up. He was sure that Erin had been less than truthful, but he couldn't imagine that Laurie had deliberately withheld information about her. She'd barely had time to ask him if he would "be so kind as to take Erin to meet Josh." But there were things going on here he knew nothing about, and it troubled him.

Will put one arm outside the sleeping bag. He couldn't get the temperature right. If he kept both arms in, it was too warm, and one arm out got frosty after a few minutes.

The moon was high and bathed his tent in soft light. Because the weather was clear, he hadn't bothered with the tent fly, but now he regretted not having the covering to hold in the heat and keep out the light.

What especially bothered him, as he ran over the events of the day, was that Laurie had talked to Erin about their relationship. He didn't like any reminders that Laurie had moved out three months previous. She had left him with little warning. He had come home to find she'd packed her things. She had told him it was just not working out like she thought it would, and she needed a break to think things over. Sounded like a bad movie. Was he so out of touch that he never suspected she was even thinking of leaving? And after two years of living together?

It had been that long since he'd been stalked by his former singing partner, Grace Diccico. She had kidnapped one of his students, Dee Tyler, daughter of the famous singer Jonathan

Tyler, on a SMOOT trip and killed her. Because Dee had dis-appeared on his watch, Will was accused of negligence. It took all of Will's skill to track Grace down, and when he did, she'd almost killed him, too.

Will had come away from the experience with a new re-spect for how much time he had left. It was then that he asked Laurie to marry him. She said she had to live with him for a while first. He settled for that, got out of running a dorm on campus for good, and that summer built a two-bedroom Cape on five wooded acres near the school.

He stuck his arm back inside the bag again, rolled onto his back, and stared up through the mesh panels at the moon.

No matter how many times he ran it through, he couldn't think of one thing he might have done to cause her to leave. She told him that although she'd been living with him for two years, she felt she knew less about him than about their cat, Gloria. It was true—at times he liked to be by himself. Just look at him now. Alone in a tent. But he'd never done anything deliberately to hurt her.

Will eventually drifted off to sleep, the night finally getting cold enough so that both arms could stay inside the bag com-fortably.

At dawn he was awakened by footfalls. At first he thought they were part of the dream where he'd been chasing after the disappearing figure that had flitted near the stand of spruce. Then he heard Erin calling his name.

He unzipped his bag and struggled out of the tent wearing only his polypro long johns. He saw Erin's flashlight. "Over here," he said. He grabbed his own light and turned it on.

She ran toward him, stumbled, and fell. "Oh, God!" she said.

Her urgent tone had the effect of stripping away sleep. He walked toward her. "What is it?" he said. "What's wrong?"

"It's Josh," she said. "I can't find him!"

———

On the trail back to the hut, Will tried to calm Erin down, but nothing seemed to help. "I just know something's happened to him," she said.

"Did you see him leave?"

"Yes. He said he was going to take a leak."

"Weren't you in separate rooms?"

She started to say something, then looked away from him.

"And what time was this?" Will said.

"About an hour ago."

Dawn light was just beginning to appear. The valley below was shrouded in mist. Could Josh have gotten lost stumbling around in the dark? Will doubted it. Not someone experienced, who'd been on the trail for so long.

At the hut he found no one stirring. He turned to Erin. "Did you tell anyone else about this?" he said.

"No. I didn't know what to do."

Will looked her directly in the eyes. "I'm sure everything is fine. I want you to stay here while I do some poking around."

"Should I tell Kevin?"

"Not yet. Just give me about fifteen minutes. Then we'll get everyone up."

Will knelt in front of the steps to see if he could pick up footprints, but the area was so impacted that he couldn't sort out any that might be Josh's. He knew that Josh had been wearing lug-soled boots with worn treads, but out here everyone opted for that sort of thing.

Despite his reassurances to Erin, he felt a clench in his throat as he began to make his way back up the trail. It didn't make sense that Josh would have ventured very far if he'd just left the hut to urinate, and it certainly wouldn't have taken an hour to empty his bladder.

Will searched the rear of the hut. The water pump wheezed as he passed it. His eyes followed the tree line, and he watched for movement. Then he headed farther up the path. He stopped, his ears pegged for sounds, but all he could hear was the rushing water.

He worked his way toward the stream, hopped over rocks, and stood on a large boulder, water rushing around him. He cupped his hands around his mouth and shouted Josh's name. Nothing.

He maneuvered his way across the stream, choosing a route that took him along the edge. He checked his bearings to make sure he knew how far he had come up from the hut and exactly where he had crossed the water to the other side.

The brush was thicker here along the stream edge, and he doubted that Josh would have bothered to go to such lengths to relieve himself. But he wanted to approach the ledges from this side so that Erin wouldn't see him. He didn't want to let her know he was even thinking that Josh might have been out near the falls.

He tried to dismiss the notion himself. Unless Josh had gotten completely disoriented, he would have known better than to venture out where it was so dangerous.

Or would he?

It struck Will suddenly that it was possible Josh didn't know anything about how steep those ledges were. Had he even known they were there? He tried to recall what Erin had said to him. They'd gone for a walk, sure, but Will guessed they had headed straight for the woods to be by themselves.

He walked slowly down to the ledges. He didn't see any footprints on the rocks leading to the falls, and that momentarily lifted his spirits. But then he noticed that the rocks themselves were damp from the morning mist. Any footprints made an hour earlier would have been covered over.

Will hesitated and looked back up toward the hut. He was sure his location was hidden from view. He felt pulled to the edge of the falls, but there seemed to be a force adding resistance. He struggled forward and peered over the edge.

Josh lay splayed out on the rocks at the bottom of the falls. One leg was twisted at an odd angle, and he wasn't moving.

Chapter 3

WILL DIDN'T KNOW HOW LONG HE'D BEEN STARING down at Josh, straining his eyes for any sign of movement, before he noticed Erin heading toward him across the ledges. He flailed his arms at her. "No. Stay there!"

She kept on coming. "What is it?" she shouted over the tumble of the water. "Have you found him?"

Will caught up to her before she could get close to the falls. "Come on. Let's go back to the hut."

She pulled away from him and studied his eyes. A shiver ran through her. "Where is he?" she demanded. Her words had a sharp, accusatory edge, as if Will had been hiding Josh all the time.

"I know where he is," Will said. "I just need to check on him."

She suddenly ripped herself away from him. Before Will could stop her, she was looking over the edge of the falls. "No!" she screamed. She held her face in both hands and dropped to her knees.

Will hesitated, for fear that any movement on his part would cause her to panic and slip over the edge. With mincing steps he approached, grabbed her shoulders, and brought her to her feet. She was dead weight.

"Let me go," she said, but she offered little resistance.

Will led her across the ledges and onto the trail to the hut. She sobbed, choking back air, rolling her head back and forth. "No!"

Will helped her walk up onto the porch. The screen door

suddenly opened for him. He was met by Jared and Marvin on their way out.

For a moment nothing happened, as both men, startled, held their ground halfway out the door.

"We've got trouble here," Will said. "I need your help."

They stepped back, and Will brought Erin inside. Kevin looked up when they came in, coffeepot suspended in mid-pour.

Will carefully placed Erin in a chair.

"How can we help?" Jared asked. Both men now looked like the soldiers they were, waiting for orders.

"It's her brother," Will said. "He's in trouble." Will wheeled to Kevin and called his name.

Kevin placed the pot on the stove, wiped both hands on his apron, and approached Will.

Will pulled him aside, out of Erin's earshot. "I need you to call in over your two-way," he whispered. "Tell them there's been an accident, a bad fall." Will paused. "What's your protocol?"

"We call Pinkham Notch. Fish and Game responds first."

"Okay. Tell them we'll assess injuries and get right back with an update."

Kevin nodded. He switched on the radio and snapped on a pair of headphones.

Will went back to Erin. She was still sobbing. Jared had his hand on her shoulder. Will knelt and spoke softly to her. "It's okay, Erin." He took her hand and held it. He thought he should say something more, but he couldn't think of any words that would comfort her.

In a few minutes, Kevin returned. "They're on their way," he said.

Will stood. "I wonder if you'd watch out for Erin, here."

Kevin nodded. "Sure."

Will hated to leave her, but he knew he had to get to Josh. He made eye contact with Jared and Marvin and motioned with his head toward the door. On the porch he explained quickly where Josh was. "The best way is to follow the trail down and then head in."

"Could you tell if he was moving?" Marvin said.

"I don't know. I don't think so."

When the three of them reached another trail that ran perpendicular, with access to the area below the falls, they left Marvin at the edge of the stream, reasoning that two men would cause less disturbance at the scene of the fall.

Will knew he'd lost precious minutes getting Erin back to the hut, but there was still a chance that Josh could be alive. But how long had he stood looking down on Josh before Erin met him at the falls? It bothered him that he had lost time—and he didn't know how much. The shock of seeing Josh in that mangled position had simply frozen him.

The water pooled below the falls, the rocks separating into wider placements, but it was still fairly easy to navigate as Will and Jared made their way in. It wasn't long before they found Josh.

Jared crouched and checked for a carotid pulse. Will studied Josh's face. There was a deep laceration on the side of his head; the blood was beginning to dry.

Jared looked up at Will. "He's dead."

"Are you sure?"

"Check for yourself." Jared stood.

Will focused on Josh's chest; there was no rise and fall. Josh looked as if he were sleeping comfortably. Will placed his hands on his hips and gazed up at the water cascading over the falls. "Don't move him, and don't touch anything," he said.

Will was surprised to find Helga Holt, not Kevin, comforting Erin. She had moved Erin to the couch and was holding her in her arms. Kevin sat quietly watching them.

Erin leaned forward at Will's entrance, her eyes red rimmed. "Is Josh okay?"

There was no easy way to do this. "I'm sorry," he said. He came to her and dropped to one knee. He took her hand again; it was wet from holding her handkerchief.

Erin said, "He's dead?"

"He had a bad fall," Will said.

"He can't be dead."

While Will was trying to think of something else to say, Erin broke down. Helga pulled her closer and stroked her hair.

Will got to his feet. It was a look of betrayal that he had read clearly in Erin's eyes, and he wondered how any of this could have been his fault. But what else could he say to her? He pulled Kevin aside and told him to call in that Josh was dead.

Now all Will had to do was wait, but he knew he couldn't do that inside the hut. He didn't want to have to say anything more to Erin. He headed out onto the porch.

On one level what had happened seemed clear to him. Josh had gone to take a leak. He became disoriented and headed toward the falls. He slipped and fell over the edge.

But something seemed wrong with the simplicity of it. Wouldn't Josh have figured out he'd gotten lost as soon as he walked onto the ledges? He certainly knew enough not to pollute his water source by urinating into it. So what was he doing there? What Will couldn't erase was the fleeting image of the figure he'd seen disappearing into the thicket. Someone else had witnessed Josh and Erin going at it and maybe had lured Josh out onto the rocks. But who? Someone in the hut? Certainly not Helga. Or Kevin. But Jared or Marvin?

It struck Will suddenly that it would have been possible for either Jared or Marvin to have followed him up from the hut when he had left to find a place to camp. And now both of them were in charge of the body. He'd better get back there.

As he headed down the trail, he met a Fish and Game officer coming up.

"You got here pretty fast," Will said.

"I came in on an ATV. You the one who made the call?"

The initials didn't register at first, and then it occurred to Will he was referring to a fat-tire, all-terrain vehicle.

Will led the man, Officer Wayne Sauvage according to his nameplate, to Josh's body. Jared and Marvin were still in their original positions, Jared near the body and Marvin along the shore. Will introduced both to Officer Sauvage.

Sauvage was lantern jawed, with a sharp pencil line of a mouth that didn't change expression. He took a look at Josh to confirm that he was dead. "I've called in the ME," Sauvage said. "No telling how long it's going to take her to get here. Someone want to tell me what happened?"

Will filled him in. He had decided before he started talking that he wouldn't mention his suspicions about the accident. He would let the facts come out, and if questions started coming up, he would chip in with his observations when the time was right. He wanted first to talk to Laurie before blabbing about anything.

Sauvage took notes and Polaroids.

Will sat on a rock looking up at the falls. Josh had landed on his side, but there was no way of telling what sort of rough and tumble had happened on his descent. If he had pitched headfirst, the gash on his head might have been a result of clipping the rough promontory that stood out just below the falls.

The more Will looked at where Josh had landed, the more he sensed something wrong. He decided to move upstream to see if he could get closer to the falls themselves.

It took some bushwhacking, and a foot-wetting tightrope walk along the edge of the stream, but he soon had the vantage point directly from the side he was seeking.

The line that Will drew in his mind's eye, the hypotenuse of the triangle from the top of the falls to where Josh's body had landed, seemed at first glance much too obtuse, but as he studied the area more closely, he realized it would be impossible to tell whether Josh had landed so far downstream because he'd nicked the outcropping of rock below the main ledge and catapulted the rest of the way—or because someone had tossed him over the edge.

State Medical Examiner Amy Liu was an athletic woman with a tight, muscular body. She'd been on the job for the past five years, and in that time she'd gained a reputation for being thorough and professional. She looked out of place with her wool car coat, but she'd at least had time to change into a pair of light hiking boots.

Will was glad to see her, gladder still when he discovered that Laurie was her escort. He suspected she would have picked up on the radio conversations. They had made the trip in along the flat trail on mountain bikes.

While the protocol called for Fish and Game to respond first, it was not an investigatory body—that was reserved for the Major Crime Unit of the state police. As a local cop, Laurie might be called in to assist, though, and being one of the first on the scene would make her an asset. Her personal stake in this, Will knew, would drive her to find the truth.

Will led Amy and Laurie to Josh's body. Officer Sauvage and Jared stepped away from Josh in deference to the woman in charge.

Liu put on a pair of latex gloves. She turned to Will. "Are you the one who found the body?"

"That's right."

"What time?"

"About six forty-five this morning. Somewhere around there."

"That's the best you can fix it?"

"It's accurate within a few minutes," Will said.

She examined Josh. "And you found the body just like this?"

"We just checked his pulse. We didn't move him." Will studied Liu as she took a look at Josh's head wound, wondering if she would betray any suspicion that this might not be an accident, but if she felt there was anything amiss, it was hidden behind her mask of efficiency.

Laurie had to turn away. Will felt like offering his comfort, but she gave little sign that she wanted him anywhere near her. As he walked with her up to the hut, he could tell she was still struggling to recover from seeing Josh's body. He decided not to say anything and follow her lead.

When they were near the porch, Laurie said, "How's Erin doing?"

"Not so hot."

"I know you've got a lot to tell me, but I need to focus on her right now," she said.

"Probably the best thing."

"Can we talk about this at the station tomorrow?"

"I'll be there."

When Erin saw Laurie enter the hut, she rose from the couch and rushed into her arms. Laurie held her, rocking her slowly. "It's okay. It's going to be okay."

Will returned to the porch so the two could be alone. He was soon joined by Helga Holt.

"Thanks for taking care of Erin," Will said.

"The poor dear," Helga said. "It's just awful. To think that young man was alive just a few hours ago . . ." She shook her head.

Will leaned against the porch railing. "When was the last time you saw Josh, Helga?"

"I heard him go outside."

"And what time was that?"

"Four thirty-five," she said without having to consider.

"How do you know for sure?"

"Because I looked at my watch after he snuck past me."

Will hesitated. "You saw him leave?"

"Walked right past me." Helga's face colored. "He didn't know that I knew."

"Knew what?"

She lowered her voice. "That he spent the night in Erin's bed."

Will nodded. He imagined Helga lying in bed getting an earful. He shifted the focus of the conversation. "Did you hear anything after he left? Anything going on outside?"

"No. I was really trying to get back to sleep."

"How about someone else leaving the hut?"

"You mean like Jared or Marvin?"

"Yes."

"No. I don't think so." She yawned. "They were snoring, I remember. The walls in this place are pretty thin. You were right to sleep outside."

"Did Erin wake you when she left to find Josh?"

"No. I guess I drifted off." She shook her head again. "It must be terrible for her, what she's going through!"

Will walked back down the trail to see if he could be of any help, but Josh's body was already secured to the small flatbed trailer that Officer Sauvage, having realized he'd probably have to haul someone out, had dragged in on the back of his ATV.

Will studied the two soldiers and again wondered if either or both had been out of the hut last night. Had Josh known these men before? Will tried to recall how they had interacted with Josh, but his only memory was seeing Josh and Erin sitting far away from them when he'd come back from pitching his tent. They weren't paying attention to each other. Will approached the two. "Thanks for you help," he said. He shook hands.

"Want us to tag along?" Jared asked.

"I think we've got it covered," Will said.

After Amy Liu called in to the lab to make sure there would be a van at the trailhead to transport the body, they moved out, Officer Sauvage driving slowly, Laurie and Erin sitting on the edge of the trailer, Amy and Will following closely behind on mountain bikes.

Chapter 4

WILL COULD STILL FEEL LAURIE'S PRESENCE IN THE HOUSE. The seemingly minor, unexpected moments cut the hardest, like opening her bureau to store the framed pictures of them together and smelling a trace of lavender soap in her underwear drawer, or discovering the missing sneaker she was so upset over losing. He never called to tell her he'd found the sneaker. It was just something he felt belonged here, and he would gladly give it back to her when she returned. It was silly, he knew, but he began to look upon the sneaker as a talisman of sorts, and as long as he kept it, there was hope for her return.

Alone now, he couldn't get rid of the image of her at the roadhead, watching stone faced as Josh's body was loaded into the van, or of her trying still to comfort Erin, who had slipped into a frightening, catatonic silence.

He sipped Laphroaig and sat back in the leather chair he hated, the replacement for his favorite overstuffed recliner with pizza stains on the arms. Getting rid of the damn, smelly thing was a concession he'd made to Laurie.

The whiskey was a mixed blessing. It helped calm Will down, but it also reminded him of Butch, his favorite cat, who had also once developed a taste for the stuff, but who'd been killed during the Grace Diccico affair. Butch had deserved a better fate. Will had gone back into the woods where Butch had died to retrieve his body and had buried him with a full, unopened bottle of Laphroaig.

He closed his eyes and remembered fondly the kids from school who had given him Gloria, a tabby, to replace Butch.

It was a touching gesture, but the cat never had taken to him as she did to Laurie, and Gloria had the good sense to move out with her.

Will's thoughts were interrupted by lights from a car in the driveway. He got up from his chair and parted the curtains. It was Laurie's cruiser.

He switched on the porch light and opened the front door. Laurie got out of the car.

"What's going on?" Will said.

"I wonder if you feel like talking now."

"Sure. Come on in."

"Can we just go for a ride?"

———

Considering that it was a Saturday night, the town of Saxton Mills was quiet, except for the dance at the teen center in the basement of the Unitarian church. Laurie drove slowly past the church, checking for kids in the bushes who might be smoking dope or nipping from pint bottles of Southern Comfort. There were none.

"I took Erin to the hospital," Laurie said. "They sedated her."

"Probably a good idea."

She turned back onto the main drag. "I'm worried, Will. She's really taking this hard."

"She didn't look good."

They drove by the main gate of the Saxton Mills School, where Will had worked for the past twenty years. He was not surprised that Laurie didn't want to wait until morning to talk with him. He understood her well enough to know that when she got antsy, she stayed up most of the night.

He'd decided when he got into the car that he would let

her ask the questions, but the silence that followed after the news about Erin in the hospital began to eat at him. He heard himself saying, "Did you know that Erin and Josh were lovers?"

Laurie pulled the cruiser over to the side of the road and parked it near the hardware store. "What on earth are you talking about?" she said.

Will told her about how "kissing your sister" had taken on new meaning, how he'd discovered them in the act.

"I had no idea," Laurie said.

"It was more than I bargained for. Incest wasn't part of the deal."

"Well, you're right." Laurie paused. "Technically it wasn't."

Will shifted in his seat and looked at her. "I figured it must be something."

"Erin is Josh's stepsister. She's my sister's daughter, but from her first marriage."

"Oh. Not technically incest." Will let out some air. "Well, I guess I feel a little better anyway."

"I swear, I never even suspected—"

"But why did you call them brother and sister?"

"Because that's the way I think of them. You're not suggesting I deliberately—"

"No, I believe you."

Laurie grew silent again. After a few moments, she said, "It must have been awful for you. I'm sorry."

"Not your fault."

She leaned her elbows on the steering wheel and let her head fall on her arms.

"You okay?" Will said.

"I don't think I can do this," Laurie said, without lifting her head. "I don't think I can take care of her."

"You're responsible for Erin?"

"By default, I guess."

"Tell me about it."

Laurie sat up straight. She wiped her eyes with her hands. "Let's drive," she said. "I think better that way."

As they made their way out of town, Laurie told Will Erin's story, how her sister Candace had married Harold Wickham, a man five years her senior whom she'd met in college. They soon had Erin. After three years of marriage, Harold became so controlling he barely let his wife and daughter out of the house. Desperate to leave the marriage, Candace sought help from a former professor, Jackson Lloyd III, aka Jacko, with whom she had a brief fling in college before meeting Harold.

"Wow. Your sister really gets around."

"She's not as loose as it sounds."

"An affair with her professor? Sounds pretty racy to me."

"She really did love Jacko. The affair ended when Kathryn, his first wife, found out about it. She filed for divorce soon after."

"Let me guess," he said. "Kathryn is Josh's mother?"

"You've got it."

"But wasn't Jacko then free to marry your sister?"

"Jacko broke off the affair with Candace after his divorce from Kathryn. He said he needed time to think. I think he got cold feet and didn't want to commit to another marriage so soon. Candace was devastated," she said.

"Enter Harold?"

"Pretty quickly. One of those rebound relationships."

"So she marries Harold, has Erin, and the guy starts dictating her life for her?"

"Candace told me he started to change after they got married. Something to do with his rediscovering God or religion. Then he turned into a control freak after Erin was born. Harold would stay up all night watching little Erin sleep to make sure she was all right. He wouldn't let Candace leave the house. Candace refused to live like that. Then he began threatening her. And one night he hit her. That was the last straw. It was terrible."

"So she turns to the one person she feels can help, her old lover Jacko."

"Candace used to sneak out and call Jacko from a pay phone. I guess their furtive conversations made Jacko remember how much he loved her, and the old fire rekindled. One night Jacko waited in his car outside the house and watched as Harold left for work. Then he spirited Candace and Erin away and set them up in a carriage house on his estate. The original plan was to provide a safe haven while she filed for divorce."

"Did Harold know where his wife and child were?"

"No. At least Candace didn't think so. As far as I know, Harold never showed up at the carriage house."

The family history opened up new questions for Will. What sorts of things went on in the carriage house before Jacko eventually married Candace? And when did Josh and Erin become lovers? Will felt like he needed a bath.

"And Erin also told me Josh was walking the AT in honor of his father," Will said.

"True."

"She said they never found Jacko's body."

"That's right, too."

"I remember you went to the service."

"Almost two years ago now. Right before I moved in with you."

He let the matter sit a moment. "You never really talked much about Jacko."

Laurie shrugged. "It is an odd situation," she said.

"You don't think Jacko was murdered, do you?"

"I try not to think about it."

"But you suspect something."

Laurie turned the cruiser around and headed back toward town. "Let's just say that the case is still open."

The dome of the sky was clear except for a haze off to the south. Will tried to weigh whether finding out that Josh was Erin's stepbrother made any difference in his feelings about her. There was no doubt she was a kid heading for trouble. He'd been working with young people long enough to know the ones with a mark, something lurking in the past that needed to be dealt with, and it was only a matter of time before disaster struck. There was no science involved with this; it was just something he knew.

"So why is Erin your responsibility? Where's your sister in all of this?"

"That's what's sad," Laurie said. "After Jacko's death she just fell apart. She's never been the same."

"You don't mean she's institutionalized?"

"No. She might as well be, though." Laurie passed the school again and turned down the road that led to the house they had shared for two years. She pulled the car into the drive. "She's agoraphobic, a virtual prisoner in the house she inherited. Ironic, isn't it? She fled Harold to regain her freedom, and now look at her."

"But she got Jacko's estate. Not bad."

"You don't understand, Will. Candace can't walk around the house without literally holding on to something. She hasn't come out since his death."

"And she lives by herself?"

"She has a helper." Laurie hesitated. "You can see why I had to get Erin away. At least try to bring back some normalcy to her life."

"I don't know if the school can do the job, though."

"I've thought about that quite a bit. Right now it's the best place for her."

Will reached for the door handle, but Laurie stayed his hand. "Thank you," she said.

"For what?"

"For being there."

Will smiled. "You ask. I jump."

On Monday morning Headmaster Perry Knowlton addressed a school assembly. He emphasized that Erin was recovering but that she would need plenty of support when she returned to the community. He described her stepbrother's accident and ended his speech with the hope that the school would not engage in any rumormongering. Any questions should be addressed to him.

The students in Will's first class after assembly seemed unaffected by the news, and it occurred to him that not many of them had really known Erin and probably found it hard, due to the short, two-week-old term, even to picture who she was.

The one exception was Erin's roommate, Kendra Mc-
Cullen, who approached Will before class began. "Are we allowed to see Erin?" Kendra asked.

"I don't think they want her to have visitors."

"Bummer."

"I guess she's feeling better, though," Will said.

"She *will* be coming back to school. That's right, isn't it,
Mr. Buchanan?"

"You heard what Mr. Knowlton said."

"I know. But . . . Erin's not dying, is she?"

"What? No. Where did you hear that?"

Kendra shrugged her shoulders.

"Why don't you take your seat. We've got work to do."

The work Will had in mind for his Wildlife Ecology
course was not in the standard high-school curriculum. One
of the reasons he had stayed at the Saxton Mills School was
that Perry had allowed him to design and teach whatever
courses he wanted.

Will looked at his attendance list. His class was made up
mostly of older students, including Berkeley Hutter, a junior.
Will remembered Berkeley's first day of school as a freshman,
when he'd found him sitting on his suitcase in the driveway,
crying his eyes out because he was lost. Berkeley had grown
about a foot since then and was still gangly as ever. He never
seemed able to catch up to his body and couldn't play sports
because of chondromalacia, a softening of the cartilage of the
knee joints. Will had noticed upon Berkeley's return for the
fall term a sparse patch of chin whiskers he'd been attempting
to cultivate.

"I want you all to gather around the table," Will said. The
chromium table he'd picked up on the cheap from the state

medical examiner's office after they'd refurbished the lab. On the table was a bone saw and a hammer and chisel. At his feet was a large cardboard carton. Will wore one latex glove on his left hand, keeping the other hand free to write on the white board. "Today we're going to learn about the life cycle of the meningeal worm."

"Sounds gastronomical." This from Leon Smith, a scholarship kid, a transferred junior, from the Bedford-Stuyvesant area of New York City. Will already loved Leon's curiosity and raw intelligence.

Will nodded. "Close. It's not a tapeworm, though." He turned to the board. "What we're dealing with here is identified as a nematode worm, a parasite that has developed a long-term relationship with the white-tailed deer."

"Like the weird uncle that moves into your house?" Leon asked.

"Exactly."

"You got a weird uncle, Leon?" Berkeley asked.

"You don't want to know."

Will turned from the board and faced the class. "What is so curious is that when this weird uncle, this parasite, moves in, there is no negative impact on the deer's overall health." He paused, deliberately, for dramatic emphasis. "For moose, though, it can cause massive damage. Sometimes this worm is the reason we see moose stumbling down the road in the middle of the town, suffering from what's commonly called 'moose sickness.' Now, what are the management implications of this?"

There was no response. Will was used to there being little give-and-take at the beginning of class. It took a while for these kids to get their synapses firing. He rephrased: "Well, it sounds to me like it's not a good idea to have moose and deer in one area, so you need to try to manage one species out. How?"

Will waited. The hardest thing for a teacher to do. In the silence Will thought of Leon's comment about the weird uncle and imagined Laurie's family, with Candace living off the host, Jacko.

"Kill all the moose?" Berkeley said finally.

The class broke into nervous laughter.

Will smiled. "Actually, Berkeley, you're not too far off. We could extend moose season to keep the numbers down."

"You mean I was right?"

"It's one solution. Or you could kill more deer. But another method would be to manage both species by creating more open areas of grazing to encourage deer and discourage moose. Moose tend to be deep-woods animals."

"But I *was* right?"

"Yes, Berkeley."

"Wait a minute," he said. "I have to mark this date on my calendar."

"You can do that after class. Right now we need to get some work done." Will pointed his grease pen at Berkeley and in a mock-serious tone said, "And stop trying to get me off track."

"Sorry, Mr. Buchanan."

"So how does this worm get into the deer?" Will asked. "Let's talk about the life cycle. Does the word 'meningeal' sound familiar?"

Silence.

"Okay, have you ever heard of spinal meningitis?"

"Doesn't it have to do with the brain?" Leon said.

"That's right. Well, the meninges are the coverings on the outer surface of the brain. If you want to know the Latin name, it is *Parelaphestrongylus tenuis.*" Will wrote the words on the board.

"Do we have to know that for the test?" Kendra asked.

"No."

"Okay, so what does a deer like to eat?" Leon asked.

"Anything it can find?" Berkeley said.

The class groaned.

"Actually, Berkeley, you're not far off again. When deer graze, they munch away on grasses and sometimes pick up snails and slugs. You've seen slugs, haven't you?"

"The orange things?" Kendra asked.

"Like jelly candy?" Berkeley asked.

"Yeah. Like that," Will said.

Leon said, "I don't know what you people are talking about."

"Well, we'll have to find some and show you," Will said. "So the deer munches on these, and some of these slugs have the encysted form of the meningeal worm inside them. Now, here's a name you do need to know."

Will wrote the word "gastropod" on the board.

"What's that?" Kendra said.

"The encysted form of the meningeal worm."

"No. I mean that word you keep using."

"Which one?"

" 'Insisted.' "

"Oh. Guess I should put that on the board, too." Will wrote "encysted" next to "gastropod." " 'Encysted' means enclosed in a cyst, which is a little sac that has fluid in it."

Kendra nodded, but the look on her face suggested he would have to offer a review session.

Will pushed on. "Now, the life cycle begins. Since it's a cycle, we can start anywhere on it, but let's say the deer eats the gastropod that's inside the snail or slug, which goes into the digestive tract and gets absorbed by the bloodstream. Then the blood takes it to the brain, and it lodges in the meninges, where it grows and becomes mature." Will diagrammed the cycle with swoops of his grease pen. "It changes to a larval form, gets back into the digestive system, is crapped out. Now, guess what happens when the slugs and snails find the pellets?"

"They eat the stuff?"

"You've got it. And they get infected with the larval form of the meningeal worm, and the cycle begins again."

"That's gross," Kendra said.

"It's Mother Nature," Will said.

"How big are these worms?" Leon asked.

Will retrieved a small bottle from a shelf and passed it around. "You can see that they are usually one to three inches in length."

"Why are they white?"

"Actually, they turn white when you stick them in the ethanol solution. When you find them in the deer's brain, they're dark. But let's see for ourselves." Will paused. "Any questions before we get started?"

Silence. Will said to Berkeley, "Will you crack those windows, please?" He put on his other latex glove. "Now, I want everyone to be as quiet and as respectful as possible."

Will reached into a cardboard box and pulled out a deer

head. He placed it on the chromium table. One eyeball dangled. Will was momentarily arrested by the sight of the deer head, preoccupied with strange thoughts about worms infesting Laurie's family tree and Jacko dead on his own property. He just couldn't stop thinking about Laurie's story.

"Oh, oh," he said, recovering. He felt the cranium. "It looks like this doe got shot in the head. The exit wound is in the eye socket. See? This brain is squash and won't do us much good, but we'll age the poor thing anyway."

Will had struck a deal with the state Fish and Game Department that he could have deer heads from roadkill and carcasses found in the wild for educational purposes. In return, each year Will reported his research to the state on the occurrence of meningeal worms in the heads he examined. Deer tested positive 60 to 70 percent of the time.

Will used a sharp buck knife with a six-inch blade to trim the skin away from the mouth. "You can age a deer by the relative pattern of wear of its premolars and molars on the lower jaw," he said. "Leon, could you get me that jaw board leaning next to the wall there?" He pointed with his knife.

Leon picked up the board, a piece of plywood with rows of deer jawbones attached, the teeth of each showing varying stages of wear.

"So how old would you guess this deer to be?" Will said.

"Two years?" Leon said.

"Everyone agree?" Will studied the class. Since he had taken the deer head out of the box, just Berkeley and Leon had kept their positions. In fact, Leon had come closer and was looking intently over Will's shoulder. The rest of the class had moved back toward the wall.

"Good guess. All this data we have to keep track of."

He placed the deer head back in the box and picked up another one. "This one looks more promising," he said. He placed the head on the table and used a bone saw to cut open the top of the deer's skull.

Kendra made a face as if she were sucking a lemon. "What's that smell?"

"Bone," Will said. "You've probably smelled the same thing in the dentist's office when you got your teeth drilled."

Will could hear the phone ringing in his office.

"Should I answer that, Mr. Buchanan?" Kendra asked.

Before Will could tell her to let it ring, Kendra ran out of the room. He didn't stop her, because he guessed she had found the excuse to leave that she'd been looking for.

Once the top of the skull was exposed, Will took his hammer and chisel and pounded hard to widen the opening to expose the meninges.

Kendra came back. "It's for you, Mr. Buchanan."

Who else would it be for? Will thought, but he didn't say it. "Can you take a message?"

"He said it was important and that he needed to talk to you."

"Did he give his name?"

"No. He just said it was important."

Will went into his office and picked up the phone. At first there was hesitation on the other end. Then, "Is the kid all right?"

"Who is this?"

"Never mind. Why is she in the hospital?"

"Erin?" Will waited a few seconds. "Could you tell me who's calling, please?"

The line went dead.

Will sat a moment, staring at the offal, the residue from the deer's brain, on his gloved hands. Then he looked up into the eyes of a stuffed fisher cat, crouching on his desk in an attitude of stealth, its coal-dark eyes unmoving, and he could almost hear its high-pitched, nocturnal scream, like the wail of an injured child.

———

Will immediately tried to get hold of Laurie, but Ray Flemmer, her deputy, said she had just left for Concord to meet with Amy Liu about the results of Josh's autopsy. Will left a message for her to get in touch with him as soon as she got back. The phone call from the stranger nagged at him, and it wasn't until after four, when Will was about to leave for the day, that Laurie showed up at his office. He immediately told her about the call.

Laurie looked stunned. "That's all he said?"

"That's it." He showed her a piece of paper. "I wrote down everything right after he hung up."

"Let's think this through." She looked around for a place to sit, but Will's office was so cramped there was barely room enough for desk and chair. They moved out into the classroom and pulled together two molded plastic chairs.

"First of all," Will said, "the caller knows who I am and where I work."

"And knows Erin."

"Enough to be concerned about her."

This habit of finishing each other's sentences had developed with their relationship. Will found himself enjoying the exchange, even though he would have preferred a different subject.

"And probably also knows that Erin went to meet Josh at the hut," Laurie said.

Was that true? He guessed it had to be, if the caller was so concerned over Erin's being in the hospital. Will figured it was about time he said what was on his mind. "I don't think Josh's death was an accident, Laurie." Will described the figure disappearing into the thicket as he was about to make camp and expressed his suspicions over the angle of the fall.

"And you're suggesting this phone call came from the guy you saw in the woods?"

"That's what I think."

Laurie stared at him for a moment, then shook her head.

Will tried to gauge her mood. He sensed the need to tread lightly. "I could be wrong. What did Liu have to say?"

"Injuries are consistent with a fall. Cause of death was a crushed skull." Laurie got up from her chair and shoved it with her foot. "God, how can kids sit in these things?" She went to a window that looked out into the woods behind the school. She arched her back, then fiddled with the string of a venetian blind. "But who would want to kill Josh?"

"Someone he met on the trail?"

Laurie turned back to Will. "Haven't there been murders of hikers on the AT? Didn't I read something about that?"

Will thought of the two girls on the southern end of the trail that had met a horrible fate. "There've been a few," he said.

Laurie crossed her arms. "Now I'm getting mad."

"Like I said, I could be wrong."

"If Josh was killed . . ." Laurie's eyes turned steely. "You know what I've been doing all morning?"

"Talking to the ME?"

"And calling relatives." She ran her hand through her hair. "God, I'm not sure I can handle this."

On an impulse Will got up and held his arms out to her. To his surprise she came to him. It felt good to hold her again.

"I can't stop thinking about Erin," she said softly, her head resting on his shoulder.

"I know."

"Will you go the funeral with me?"

"Of course."

Holding her, he could smell her lavender soap. "I've missed you," he said.

"Me, too." She gently broke the embrace. She gave him a pat on the shoulder. "What's your schedule look like tomorrow?"

"Same old. Lunch with the queen, that sort of thing."

She smiled. "Feel like taking a hike after classes?"

"Where to?"

"I want you to show me where you camped. Take another look at the falls. I want to get the scene in my head before I ask the Major Crime Unit to get involved."

———

It was Kevin's day off. His replacement was a recent graduate of Tufts University who was biding her time until she got accepted to law school. Virginia Stoltz made Will feel uncomfortable because she was always smiling. Her teeth were cotillion white, as perfect as her bubbly mood. She was obviously going to be little help to them.

On the way up the trail to the spot where Will had

camped, he said to Laurie, "It's too bad Kevin's not here. You might want to follow up with him."

"What are you thinking?"

"I'd be curious to find out what happened to Jared and Marvin after we left."

"Those are the two army guys?"

"Marines. The ones I left with Josh's body."

"You think they might have been involved?"

Will stopped to get his bearings. "If you find out that they knew Josh beforehand, then you'd probably want to talk with them." Will went off trail, and Laurie followed.

"Why is it I always seem to end up in the woods with you?" Laurie said.

"Because you like being around me."

She let the line drop. "Is this where you camped?"

"In the birch stand. Josh and Erin were going at it over there." Will parted branches and stepped into a small clearing. "Right here."

Laurie shook her head. "I don't know. Kids seem to grow up pretty fast these days."

"Promise me you won't say that again," Will said.

"Why?"

"I just get sick of hearing it." He searched the area for footprints but found none. There was some evidence of broken-off, shoulder-height twiggy branches on a large spruce near the trail, indicating that someone might have brushed by. It only confirmed what he already suspected: He had seen someone there.

Will led Laurie across the stream, following the path he'd taken on his search for Josh. A mist had settled in, the air so heavy with moisture he could taste it on his lips. As they reached the open spot near the falls, it began to rain steadily, and Will put the hood of his poncho over his head. "Not the best day to be out here," he said.

"I know. Thanks for humoring me."

"Had enough?"

"Is there a way to get down from this side?"

"I don't think so. The trail by the hut is the only way I know of."

"You never took a look from this side?"

The water dripped off his hood, and Will shook himself like a wet dog. "You want me to go down this way, don't you."

"I just thought . . ."

"It's really true. You *are* trying to kill me."

Laurie looked over the edge where Josh had fallen. "Forget it. It doesn't look safe. Especially in this rain."

Will walked to the side and noticed a small path he hadn't seen before. "Looks like someone's been down this way, though." He followed the overgrown path. It wound away from the ledge and then circled back about ten feet below the falls. He looked up and could see Laurie peering down at him. "Be careful!" she yelled.

From this location he could look down and more clearly see the outcropping where he speculated Josh first clipped and then catapulted himself into space. The water rushed and roared by his head. There was a way to continue down over the ledge, but it would be tricky going, not something he was about to attempt in this sort of weather.

As he turned to make his way back up the trail, his eye caught something to his left. It was a watch.

Later, over tea in the hut, Will examined it. A well-worn Rolex. The lens was shattered.

Laurie shook her head. "Amazing," she said.

"What is?"

"What you're able to find in the woods. Most people would have passed right by it."

She was referring to Will's penchant for "found art." Their house was crammed full of driftwood and gewgaws Will had discovered over the years. He had a drawerful of rusted jack-knives he'd found in the field.

Will's brow knitted. "What do you suppose this is doing out here?"

"Obviously somebody lost it."

"But why wear such a fancy thing into the woods? It's got to be worth a few grand."

"Or more. I get what you're saying. It's not your typical field watch."

"You should keep it as evidence."

Laurie took out a plastic bag and opened it. "Stop handling it, then. Your prints are all over it by now."

He put the watch down on the arm of his chair. "Sorry."

"This isn't your way of trying to score an expensive watch, is it?" Laurie positioned the plastic bag next to the edge of the chair arm, and, using her ballpoint pen, poked the watch into the bag. She held the bag up to the light. "Oh, look at that." She used her pen as a pointer.

It took a moment for Will to realize it was the condition of the band she was referring to: broken, not at the clasp nor the pin but at a link.

Chapter 5

THE FUNERAL FOR JOSH LLOYD WAS SPARSELY AT-
tended, held at a small Episcopal church near his father's
property, which bordered the White Mountain National
Forest near Campton. After the service the cortege processed
to the family burial plot, located on a knoll where Josh's
grandmother and grandfather had already taken up afterlife
residence.

The sun glared off the water in the distance. The pond below the knoll was the same one where Jacko's canoe had been
found floating empty and where, after much dragging and
searching, his body had never been discovered.

Just a few hundred yards north of the knoll, somewhere in
the vast confines of the house, Laurie's distraught sister was
hiding behind curtains, moving about by leaning against walls
and grabbing onto chairs, unable to attend the ceremonies
because the fear of wide-open spaces had become her prison.

Will was surprised there were few younger people of Josh's
age in attendance, except for Erin, who had managed to control her grief through most of the church service as she
leaned against the shoulder of another youth in dreadlocks
sporting a crocheted Rastafarian headpiece that looked like a
hornet's nest.

"Who is that with Erin?" Will whispered to Laurie.

"Never saw him before."

Birch leaves littered the ground near the grave site. Will
didn't think much of ceremonies that tended to make the
dead larger than they were in life. It was dust to dust, and
there was nothing much more to say about it. He focused on

leaves flying as a gust of wind picked them up, conscious of Laurie's arm hooked through his, the light downward pressure every now and again as she struggled to maintain equanimity.

Mourners stepped forward to place roses on Josh's coffin, and soon he was lowered into the ground. Will approached the grave with Laurie. He tossed dirt into the hole and said a few words to himself.

Afterward Laurie introduced Will to Josh's mother, Kathryn, who'd been watching the ceremonies expressionless, as if Josh had been a distant relative instead of a beloved son. Will knew better than to make judgments, knowing well the individual nature of grief.

"Laurie has told me about you," Kathryn said. "I want to thank you for all that you've done."

"I haven't done much of anything, Mrs. Lloyd." Will took her hand. "I'm sorry about your loss."

Kathryn managed a smile, then turned. "I'd like you to meet Josh's brother, Mr. Buchanan. He's flown in all the way from Las Vegas." She said this as if it were a minor miracle.

Will shook hands. Jackson Lloyd IV's hair was gel-coiffed and slicked back straight over his head. He was lanky and slump shouldered, dressed in a tailored, chalk-striped, charcoal gray business suit. There was a milky, alcoholic film to his eyes that suggested an air of lofty indifference. "Nice to meet you," he said, but something in the tone made Will suspect his sincerity.

At the reception, held in the basement of the Episcopal church, Will talked with Laurie about the older brother. "Is he some sort of snob or what?"

"Not really. More a black sheep."

Will took a bite of a finger sandwich. "The prodigal son?"

She looked around to see if anyone was listening and lowered her voice. "The hell-raiser, ex–drug pusher anyway. When his father found out about his cocaine habit, he virtually disowned him."

Across the room Jackson was standing by himself, looking impatient to leave. Will's eye caught Erin huddled with Kathryn and recalled her talking about Josh's inheritance as if it were a burden. "So you're saying Jackson was cut out of Jacko's will?"

"Well, yes and no. I think his father still loved him despite everything." She took a sip of her punch. "But he changed his will, skipped over Jackson, and made Josh next in line. If anything should happen to Josh, though, the inheritance would go back to Jackson."

"But if Jackson was a rotten son, why would he even be considered to get anything?"

"Jacko wanted to keep the assets in the family. Much of his estate involves land, valuable land that borders the national forest; he knew he needed a good caretaker. Josh had a good business head."

"And Jackson doesn't?"

"I guess he was hoping that Jackson would change with the years."

Will thought about the two brothers. It's no wonder that Josh considered the inheritance as a heavy weight. "So what did Jackson do after this big blowout with his father?"

"He moved to Las Vegas."

"Well, I know that much. I meant, here he is in line to inherit valuable land, and his younger brother leapfrogs over him. He must have been miffed."

"He was."

"Did he leave quietly?"

"I really don't know." Laurie refilled her punch glass. "All I know is that the will stipulated that if Josh's father died before Jackson turned his life around, what was originally to be his would fall to Josh on his twenty-first birthday."

"A milestone he sadly won't reach."

"I still can't believe he's dead." She touched Will's hand. "Thanks for coming with me." The second time she'd thanked him in a week.

He grabbed her hand and squeezed it. "Come back to the house, Laurie. We can make it work."

"Why do you always do this?"

"What?"

"See any sign of my appreciation as an opening."

"Because I want you back. I'm looking for anything."

"We'll talk."

"Talk? What's to talk about?"

"Whatever we have to talk about, we'll talk about later." She let go of his hand. "Now I think we should mingle."

"Wait a minute. I have a question."

"I said, I don't want—"

"It's not about us, it's about Erin."

"What about her?"

"Is she coming back with us?"

"She'll be staying with Kathryn until she feels well enough to return to school."

"Kathryn? They get along well?"

"Well enough. I just think it's important for Erin to get away for a while."

"Thanks." Will held out his hands as if to show her he

hadn't been hiding anything. "See? That's all I wanted to know." He watched her walk away. He always liked to watch her walk.

He stopped at the table and decided the only mingling he would do was with another finger sandwich. Egg salad was his favorite.

As he ate, he sifted through what he'd learned from Laurie about the inheritance. What had remained unspoken was the realization that if someone had a good reason for wanting Josh dead, it was his older brother.

————

Will and Laurie had just left the church and were about to get into her Cherokee when they were approached by the young man with the Rastafarian headgear who had stood by Erin during the ceremony.

"Excuse me," he said. "Are you Mr. Buchanan?"

"That's right."

"Erin thinks I should talk with you."

Will and Laurie exchanged glances. She gestured toward the church. "Want to go back inside?"

"Out here's good."

"What's your name?" Laurie asked.

He hesitated and glanced at Will. "This is Officer Eberly," Will said. "Erin's aunt."

"Officer? You a cop?"

"That's right."

He made a show of pulling himself up straight and hitching his pants. "Name's Zippy."

"Zippy?" Will echoed.

Zippy grinned at him. "My trail name. Jimmy Montroy's the real one." He nodded at Laurie. "For the record."

"What's a trail name?" Laurie said.

"You know, when you hike the AT, you get a trail name. Josh's was 'Dark Star.' "

"You hiked with Josh?" Will said.

"For a while, yeah."

The news brought Will up short. Here was someone who might be able to shed light on events that led up to Josh's fall. Laurie said, "Why don't we go over here." She headed toward a hillock that had been newly raked and sat down. Will joined her. The coolness of the grass startled him as he sat. Zippy sat cross-legged in front of them.

"Why was Josh called 'Dark Star'?" Will asked.

"I guess 'cause he was always kind of serious, you know what I mean?"

"I didn't know him that well," Will said.

"No? The way Erin talked, I figured . . ."

"What did she say?" Laurie asked.

"Made it sound like Buchanan here was her best bud. Naturally figured he should know Josh pretty good."

Will shifted the conversation. "So what can we do for you, Zippy?"

Zippy picked at the grass. "I don't know. I guess I got some questions about stuff."

He picked some more grass. Will could tell he was thinking about how to frame his "stuff," but he was having trouble making connections.

"Stuff, like, you know," Zippy continued, "how did he fall like that? I mean, it doesn't make any sense, you know what I mean?"

"Why doesn't it make sense?" Laurie said.

"It just doesn't, man!"

Will wondered how much dope Zippy had smoked in his life. He had to find a way to cut through the haze. "Zippy. Do you have something specific you want to tell us?"

Zippy looked up at Will. His eyes were veined in red. "I think someone was following us, man."

"On the trail? Someone was following you?" Laurie repeated.

"That's right. I think he offed Josh."

"Did you see this guy?" Will asked.

Zippy looked like he was thinking real hard. "I didn't. Josh said he did."

"And you think this guy killed Josh?" Will said.

"Yeah. That's what I said."

Will ignored his annoying tone. He was still trying to measure how stoned Zippy might be.

"When did you first notice you were being followed?" Laurie asked.

"About a week ago, I guess."

"How come you weren't with Josh at the hut?" Will asked.

"He was moving too fast for me. I like to take my time. I dropped down a few days before for supplies, and he split to meet up with Erin." He slapped his hands together. "Whoosh," he said. "Man, he was in a hurry to get his horns clipped, you know what I mean? All he could talk about."

Laurie took a small pad from her hip pocket. "So, if I understand it right, you say Josh thought he was being followed, but you never saw anyone?"

"That's right."

"But Josh did?"

"That's what he said. Goddamn. Didn't I just tell you that?"

"Bear with me," Laurie said.

"Anybody can see you don't go taking a leak off a fuckin' cliff, you know what I mean?"

"Suppose he didn't know it was there?" Will suggested.

Zippy cocked his head and closed one eye. "Oh, he knew it was there all right. He knew where everything was." He paused. "If it was me, I might have fallen off the cliff, but not Josh."

Zippy's disclosure brought to mind again the figure Will had seen disappearing into the spruce grove. Now, for the first time, he had corroboration, shaky though the source might be, that there had been someone out there who knew Josh's every move.

"Question for you, Zippy."

"Go for it."

"Did Josh wear a watch?"

"What?" Zippy grinned. "Whoa. That was random." He paused. "No. You don't need no watch in the woods."

Laurie put her pad away. "Is there anything else you'd like to tell us, Zippy?"

"I just got a question for you." He rolled to the side, got his feet under him, wavered, then spread them wider for support. He stared at Laurie. "What the hell are you going to do about it?"

"Did you tell Erin you thought Josh had been killed?" Laurie said.

"Of course. That's why she wanted me to talk to you. Why?"

"I just wanted to know."

"Well . . ."

" 'Well' what?"

"What are you going to do about it?"

Laurie got up and brushed the back of her pants. "I appreciate the information, Mr. Jimmy Montroy, aka 'Zippy,' or whoever the hell you are. I think the first thing I'm going to do is run a background check on you to see what it says. Previous arrests, that sort of thing."

Zippy let out a low whistle. "Makes sense. Cops are always going after the wrong guy."

"I do want to thank you for being there for Erin, today, though," Laurie said, managing a smile. "It obviously meant a lot to her."

He returned her smile, but it was forced. "A pleasure."

"How long have you known Erin?" Will asked.

"Just met her. Weird chick."

———

It turned out that Zippy did have a record for peddling drugs and had done some time in a Pennsylvania county pen. Laurie told Will this on Sunday, a week after the funeral, in the car on their way to Kathryn's to pick up Erin.

"I checked it out, the watch," Will said. "It's worth about twenty-five hundred."

"And?"

"And I can't stop thinking about it. Who the hell wears an expensive Rolex into the woods?"

"Good question. And what do you make of Zippy's story about being followed?" she said.

"Why would he lie?"

"I don't know. I just don't trust him." Laurie drove with both hands on the wheel, her arms rigid.

"Were you able to find anybody who saw him when he dropped down for supplies?"

"I followed up with the general store he says he visited, but nobody remembers him."

Will pondered this a moment. "So you think *he* might be the one I saw in the woods?"

"It makes sense, doesn't it? He knew Josh, he was already in the woods, and he had every opportunity to follow along behind."

"But why would Zippy shove his friend over the falls?"

"I don't know. Maybe they had an argument. You know how things get blown out of proportion on the trail."

"Do you really believe that?"

"Just playing devil's advocate." She kept her eyes on the road, and the only thing they shared for a few moments was the hum of the tires. Then she turned her head toward Will. "I do know this, though. Most murderers know their victims."

She said this with such conviction that Will wasn't sure whether she was ever going to look at the road again. He nodded and motioned with his head toward the highway.

She finally concentrated on her driving again, leaving Will to wonder who else might have known the victim, and he couldn't get rid of the idea that Jackson IV had more of a reason than Zippy did to have Josh dead. It had bothered him all week long.

"What are you thinking about?" Laurie said.

"Motive."

"And . . . ?"

"Suppose Zippy did kill Josh, but someone put him up to it."

"Like who?"

"Jackson?"

"Like I said before, I don't think Jackson would kill his own brother."

"Not even *have* him killed?"

"No. It just doesn't feel right."

"Answer me this, then. If Zippy was guilty for any reason, why would he have bothered to pull us aside and tell us he thinks Josh was murdered? I mean, wouldn't he want to argue that it was an accident?"

Laurie didn't have an immediate answer. "I just don't trust the guy," she said finally.

Kathryn Lloyd lived about fifty miles southwest of Saxton Mills, in the trendy community of New London, which boasted the highest percentage of millionaires in New Hampshire. By the looks of the house, a recently constructed, custom-built Cape on land overlooking Pleasant Lake, Kathryn had done pretty well by her divorce. As soon as Laurie's Cherokee headed up the driveway, Will could see Erin coming out of the house to greet them.

Laurie got out of the car, and Erin rushed to embrace her. To Will's surprise he was next in line. Erin threw her arms around his neck and kissed him on the cheek. Her perfume smelled like rose petals.

"I'm sooo glad to see you two," Erin said.

Laurie looked at the house. "Where's Kathryn?"

"Church."

"And you didn't go?"

"I've had enough of God for a while," Erin said.

———

They waited an hour for Kathryn's return, but she didn't show. Laurie left a note. On the ride back, Will sat in the rear to give Laurie and Erin a chance to talk, but a half hour into the trip, Erin fell asleep. Will was grateful for the brief turn-around at Kathryn's because he still had classes to prepare. He'd seen more of Laurie in the last few weeks than he had in the whole three months since she'd moved out, and, as painful as Josh's death had been, the one good that might come of it was that he and Laurie might soon be back to-gether. Will could tell, though, watching Laurie from the backseat, that she was tense, probably feeling the burden of having Erin back in her care again. This was not a responsi-bility that would go away soon.

Back at the Saxton Mills School, Kendra, Erin's room-mate, looked up from her desk and let out a shriek when Erin entered the room. The two girls hugged each other.

"Oh, my God!" Kendra said. "You're back! I had no idea you were coming."

"I made up my mind yesterday. Sorry, I should have called."

Will smiled to himself as he brought in Erin's suitcase, mo-mentarily thinking about the resiliency of the human spirit. Right now he was sure the best place for Erin was right in this room with Kendra.

"Oh, I'm so sorry," Kendra said. She brought her hands to her mouth. "I wish I could say something that would help."

Erin held on to her. "It's all right. You don't have to say anything. I'm better. I really am."

"Are you sure?" Laurie asked. "You're really ready to come back?"

Erin reached for Laurie and brought her into a three-way hug. "I'm ready," she said.

All this hugging made Will feel the odd man out. He walked over to Erin's bureau and leaned against it. He stared

at his shoes, then shifted his weight and looked back toward
the bureau. On it was a picture of Josh and Erin that looked
as if it had been taken recently. Josh had one arm around her
shoulder, and she was holding on to it. The picture evoked in
Will sadness over a life cut short, but there was something else
troubling about it that he couldn't identify at first. He studied
it and then realized there was one detail that seemed out of
place: Josh was wearing a watch. Erin's hand was partially
covering it, but from the metal band and what he could see of
the face, it looked remarkably like the Rolex he'd found.

Chapter 6

OUTSIDE THE DORMITORY LAURIE LEANED AGAINST THE porch pillar.

"You okay?" Will asked.

"I think so. I just need to catch my breath."

Will touched her shoulder. "It's been quite a few weeks."

Laurie's faced suddenly changed. In their two years of living together, Will could count on one hand the number of times she had cried, and now her tears came as a shock.

He held her. "It's okay," he said. "Just let it come."

Her body shuddered as she sobbed. It was so unlike her to react this way that it scared him. He'd been eager to tell her about his discovery of Josh's wearing a watch in the photograph, but under the circumstances it could wait.

It took a minute or so, but she drew herself away, wiping her eyes with her sleeve. "I don't know what got into me."

He handed her his handkerchief. "Come on," he said. "Let's get a drink."

The Burger & Brew was the only show in town, a haunt Will knew well. He checked his watch. The place closed at five on Sunday. They had a little over an hour.

As Will drove her Cherokee, Laurie said, "I guess it was a combination of things. I'm sorry."

"You don't have to apologize. You can't help the way you feel."

"But I've put you through so much already. You don't need me blubbering on top of everything else."

Will pulled into the parking lot of the Burger & Brew. He

stopped the car and placed his arm over the seat. "Look, Laurie. This is what happens to people. They get upset."

Because the Burger & Brew charged nearly four bucks a pop for Laphroaig, Will usually settled for draft beer, but tonight he called for the good stuff. Laurie ordered a Manhattan.

"I'm so sorry I dragged you into this," she said.

"You didn't. It happened, that's all."

She took a sip from her drink, leaned back in her chair, and sighed. "It's just my stupid family. I should have gone with Erin to the hut."

"You were busy, remember?"

"I could have adjusted my schedule."

"But you didn't."

She cocked her head. "Why are you so understanding about this?"

"You don't live with someone for so long without feeling a responsibility for her."

She stared at him a moment. "That was nice," she said. "Thank you."

"You're welcome." The whiskey burned his throat. It was the musty aftertaste he loved, and he savored it as he studied her hands. Her fingers were long and delicate, a soft feature that belied her tough exterior. He loved the way she touched him. It seemed a distant memory.

"I did check on your two soldiers," she said.

"My what?"

"Jared and Marvin."

"Oh, yeah."

"Nothing points to their having known Josh before the incident."

"I see."

"Well, you did want me to look into that, right?"

"Yeah, sure."

She leaned forward. "Something wrong?"

His eyes moved from her hands to her face. He was reminded of why he was first attracted to her, the way her dark hair offset her light skin, how the tiny laugh lines by her eyes came together when she smiled. "Sorry, guess I was thinking about something else." He couldn't get the photograph of Josh out of his mind, but even though she had started talking about the case, he didn't want the subject of Josh's watch to upset her more or dominate the conversation. Besides, he wanted to talk about them.

"For a minute there, you looked as spaced-out as Zippy," she said.

"A little tired, I guess." He ordered another Laphroaig.

Laurie placed her hand over the half-consumed Manhattan. "None for me, thanks." She reached into her glass, pulled out the cherry, and put it in her mouth.

Will watched her eat it.

"I'm sure a lot of this emotion was brought on by my brother Peter," she said. "I'm so disappointed in him."

"Your brother? What's wrong?"

"You know he's a land developer, right?"

"I didn't."

"Well, he's had his eye on this property that Josh was to inherit for a long time. It's right near Loon Mountain."

"Loon? The homestead's in Campton."

"There are two parcels. Peter is looking into that part of the package as a potential ski area. He's already had some people walking the property."

"And Loon? More condos?"

"A shopping center, I think. Anyway, he was courting Jackson all week. I mean, here's Josh barely in the ground while Peter is trying to lure Jackson into selling the property."

"Was Peter at the funeral? I don't remember seeing him."

"No. He was too busy." She shook her head. "He's so callow."

"I'm sure you'll set him straight."

It really was quite a family that Laurie came from—an agoraphobic sister, a niece who just lost her lover/stepbrother, and now a brother without a heart. What had Laurie's parents been like? In all their two years of living together, Laurie had hardly mentioned them. Will sat forward in his chair. This seemed as good a time as any to bring up what had been bothering him since Erin first walked on the scene.

"What's the matter?" she asked.

He pushed his drink forward and rested his elbows on the table. "I need to run this by you. Tell me if I'm wrong."

Laurie chewed the end of her swizzle stick. "Sounds serious."

Will cleared his throat. "Your moving out a few months ago corresponds, I think, with Erin's coming on the scene, right?"

"Right."

"You know what I think happened?"

"I imagine you're going to tell me."

"I think you got scared. Here you were, suddenly taking on responsibility for Erin. You couldn't see her living at the house. So you left."

Laurie thought a moment. "I don't think it happened quite like that," she said.

"Tell me where I'm wrong."

"You make it sound too simple."

"But I am right that Erin had a lot to do with your leaving?"

Laurie downed the rest of her Manhattan. "Yes, you're right, of course. I know I didn't want you to have to deal with my problem."

"That's great!"

"What?"

"Don't you see? That means it's not all my fault."

She fingered the stem of her glass. "I never thought that. I told you I had some things to work out for myself, and I did."

"But you also mentioned living with me for all this time and not knowing me better than Gloria. Like it was all my fault."

"Well, I still think I don't know you that well. You never say much to me about anything real."

"And don't you think I could claim the same? My God, Laurie! The stuff I've learned about you and your family in the last week is more than I have in two years."

"I'm sorry. I guess I screwed things up."

"So that means you'll come back? I mean, Erin's in school now. It's not like she's living with you."

Laurie hesitated. "Give me some time. Let's see how she settles in. She may want to move back with me." Tears began to well up again in her eyes. "Can I have another drink?" she asked.

It took some convincing, because last call had already been given, but Will had always been a good customer, and soon they were the only ones left at the bar.

"It's more than just Erin coming into my life," Laurie said. "It's about where I am."

"And where's that?"

"Between here and there, I guess." She played with the cherry in her glass. "I'm not really sure I can say exactly what I mean, but I'm going to give it a shot, okay?"

"Please. Go ahead."

"Erin forced me to think about us—you're right. I suddenly felt claustrophobic, and I didn't know why. I knew you deserved an explanation, but I really didn't have a clue about what to tell you, because I didn't understand it myself." She drank a little and placed the glass carefully back on the table. "Stop me if this gets too weird."

"Keep going."

"So I took the coward's way out. I didn't say anything for fear I would say something wrong." She reached across the table and touched his hand. "It's pretty lame."

"You know what I think?"

"No."

"I think Erin's coming into your life was also a reminder that your relationship with me was getting too serious and if we weren't careful, we might end up like your—what did you call them?—your 'stupid family'? You should have talked to me about it."

"I know. Maybe we just shouldn't be together."

"You really believe that?"

"Well, we've been living together for two years, and it's obvious we still don't talk to each other. I mean, you're right. I'm probably just as closed up about things as you are."

"Then why do I still love you?"

She stared at him for a moment. "You love me?"

"Of course I do."

She sat back in her chair. She let her hands rest on the arm and stared straight ahead.

"What's the matter?" he asked.

"Nothing."

"Don't do that, Laurie. Tell me what you're thinking. Don't get quiet on me now."

"It's just that I don't think I can remember you saying you loved me before."

"I know I've said that before."

"Not like that. Not just coming out with it. Not saying 'I love you' just like that."

"But, I *have*."

She leaned forward. "No you haven't."

"Yes I have."

"Have not."

He touched her fingers. "Sleep with me."

"No."

"We need to be together tonight."

"I can't. I feel too vulnerable."

"You're supposed to feel vulnerable. That's the idea."

"Please, Will."

"Are you sure?"

She finished her Manhattan and met his eyes. "No."

————

Gloria the cat greeted them with several meows. Will stroked her behind the ears, and she arched her back. Then she ran away from him. Laurie had taken an apartment at Marchesi Meadows. The place brought back bad memories for Will. He had been holed up in one of the Meadows' crummy apartments after he'd lost his job a few years back because he was suspected of having killed Dee Tyler, one of his students, when all the while it had been Grace Diccico.

On the way over to her apartment, Laurie had agreed to sleep with him under one condition: He was not to say one thing. No talking.

At first Will considered the no-talking rule weird, but there was something unexpectedly sensuous in his being able to communicate only with his hands. Even though Laurie hadn't told him why, he understood that being silent meant there was no chance that either of them might say anything that would mess up the moment.

He picked her up in his arms, carried her into the bedroom, and placed her gently on the bed. He turned off the light on the side table, but she switched it on again. It was a gesture, perhaps a giving up of her vulnerability, for Will knew well her preference for darkness. This turned him on more than anything.

He stripped and stood before her.

She started to take her clothes off, but he stopped her. He removed her shoes first and massaged her toes. She lay back on the bed, one arm resting over her head. With her clothes still on, he ran his hands gently up one leg. He lay next to her, placed a hand on her breast, and could feel her heart pounding, her hot breath on his ear. He unbuttoned her blouse and helped her off with her jeans.

He kissed her belly. She made a whimpering sound, and Will smiled at her. He put a finger to her lips, as if admonishing her for making a noise.

They lay touching each other afterward, and Will fell asleep. He woke hours later and found Laurie on top of him, gently urging him to wakefulness. As she moved her body slowly, he reciprocated, sensing the rhythm she wanted, and in that moment he felt sure that what Erin had said that day he walked in with her to Zealand Falls Hut was true, that Laurie had been sad over their separation and that she truly had missed him.

At first light Will sensed that he should leave before she woke for fear he might say something wrong.

––––––

Before leaving for school that same morning, Will called Laurie from their house. "I'm imagining you smiling," he said. "Yes?"

Laurie yawned. "Why did you leave?"

"Mime sex was just too good to talk about."

"Mime sex?"

"I think we should let Dr. Ruth know we're onto something." He hesitated. "Miss me?"

"Of course."

"Then you are smiling."

"I'm smiling."

"That's all I wanted to know."

"Wait a minute. Don't hang up."

"I'm here."

"Keep an eye on Erin for me?"

"Goes without saying."

There was a pause on the line. "No. Forget it. I'm really sorry about this. This isn't your problem. You don't have to do anything if you don't want to."

"You keep saying you're sorry. I'm sorry that you're sorry, but please don't say that you're sorry again."

Laurie laughed. "Sorry," she said.

There was a playfulness in her voice that he hadn't heard for a while, and it lifted his spirits.

"Last night was good," she said.

Will felt a rush of heat on his neck. He'd heard what he had hoped for. Last night was good. He wanted to freeze the moment, and he couldn't think of anything to say, which was probably a good thing. Learning to shut up might just be the best way of improving communications in their relationship. "I know," he said. "We shouldn't talk about it, though."

"Oh, yeah. Mum's the word."

"Not true."

"No?"

"Mime's the word."

Chapter 7

RECONCILING WITH LAURIE HAD HELPED PUSH JOSH'S death temporarily into the background of Will's thinking, but watching Erin move about the school during the day—studying her reactions in assembly, catching her for a chat in the lunchroom—brought back the nagging unanswered questions.

The familiar surroundings of his office reminded him of the strange phone call, and he found himself between classes staring at the phone, expecting it to ring. Who had been on the other end? And the photograph of Josh. Zippy had told them that Josh hadn't worn a watch, and yet there he was with his arm around Erin, resplendent in an expensive Rolex.

Will finally told Laurie about the photograph on Monday morning. She immediately went to Erin's room and asked her if it would be all right if she borrowed it to make a copy.

Laurie stopped by the school on Tuesday afternoon with the news that the only discernible prints on the Rolex he'd found belonged to him.

"Sorry about that."

"We found something else, though. There's alphanumeric stuff on the inside of the casing. It looks like a code."

"You're kidding."

"Here." She handed him a slip of paper: 10JL2102JL358.

"So what does it mean?"

"I don't know. I've talked to the Major Crime Unit about what we've discovered. They're considering an investigation."

He thought a moment. "But that's good news, isn't it? That they're thinking about opening a case."

"I guess so. But such good news I don't need. I'd sleep better if I knew it had been an accident."

Will took another look at the numbers and letters on the paper. "Wait a minute. You don't suppose the 'JL' here means 'Josh Lloyd,' do you?"

Laurie took a long look at the paper. "But why two JL's?"

"I don't know. Seems like too much of a coincidence for the letters to correspond with his initials and not be his." He handed her back the piece of paper. "I mean, what are the odds?"

"So the watch belongs to Josh after all?"

Will nodded. "Which means Zippy was lying."

"It could mean that." Laurie rubbed her neck with her hand. "Maybe Zippy just didn't know about the watch. Maybe Josh just didn't wear it on the trip."

"Then how did it get there?"

Laurie didn't have an answer.

———

As the week progressed, Erin seemed to settle in to the routine of school life, and Will grew less worried about her adjustment. He knew it was selfish, but he was hoping for a return to normalcy so that he could persuade Laurie to move back in. She seemed more at ease around him lately, suggesting that there had been positive effects of their night together. If he just bided his time, he was sure she would return home, especially if she felt Erin was safe at school.

On Saturday, two weeks from the day that he'd led Erin in to meet Josh at Zealand Falls, Will spent most of the morning working a chain saw on a wooded area of the school property that had been severely damaged by last winter's ice storm.

Part of Will's rather lengthy job description involved the

management of the two thousand acres of forest the school owned. When he first began working for Saxton Mills, this had been his sole responsibility, and it was only through the years that he gradually added more teaching duties. Will had a degree in forestry from UNH, but much of his hands-on skill had come from the years he'd spent as a youth helping his grandfather manage a thousand-acre tree stand in Canada.

The tree work was particularly dicey, what with the ice-twisted birches, because the direction of fall was difficult to predict. The danger of widow-makers, overhanging branches that could break off, was also real, so Will had to watch over-head and concentrate with extreme care. By noon he was exhausted, but it was a good feeling. The work had taken his mind off Josh. As he sat on a stump and wiped his brow with a bandanna, he was surprised to see Erin making her way up the trail.

She hailed him, and he waved back.

"How did you find me?" he asked as she approached.

"I asked around."

"Everything all right?"

"Not really."

"What's wrong."

"I want to switch advisers."

"Who do you have now?"

Erin put her hands on her hips and caught her breath. "Miss Parmalie."

A geometry teacher in her forties, Ellen Parmalie was spindly legged, with a large, out-of-proportion upper torso. "What's wrong with her? She's a nice person."

"She may be nice, but she doesn't have a clue."

"You might consider giving her a chance. You've only known her a short time."

"I don't have to. I just don't like her." Erin smiled at Will. "What are those things you're wearing?"

Will slapped his leg. "These?"

"Yeah, those."

"Chaps. They protect you in case the saw wants to take a bite."

"Wow. Lucky saw."

"What?"

"Nothing."

Will shifted on the stump. What the heck was going on? Was she actually flirting with him?

"Would you be my adviser, Mr. Buchanan?"

Will hesitated. "I don't think that would be a good idea."

"Why not? You know me the best on this campus. I think you could help me more than Miss Parmalie."

Will scratched his head. "Don't you think you'd be able to relate to a woman better?"

She pouted and turned on her heels.

"Wait a minute," Will said. He put his hand on her shoulder, and she whirled and fell into his arms.

"Please," she said. "I'll be good. I promise." She hugged him tight.

He let his arms drop to his side. "It's okay. Look . . ."

"You're just so nice to hold."

Will tried to undo her arms from around his middle, but she clutched him tighter.

"Erin! Let go of me!" She slowly relaxed her grip, and he held her out at arm's length. "Now, I don't want you to do that to me again."

"I just gave you a hug."

"You're not supposed to just give me a hug."

"Why? Because you're a teacher?"

"A hug like that from you isn't meant for a teacher."

"But you're more than that, aren't you? You and Aunt Laurie will probably get married someday." She touched his arm. "That makes us almost related. Like kissing cousins."

"I don't think so."

"Can't you just be my adviser?"

"We're going back to school. We can talk about this on the way down."

———

The more Will tried to convince Erin that he would make a lousy adviser, the more she dug in her heels. Will called Laurie and expressed his concern.

"Don't you think Erin's just reaching out to you for support?" she asked.

"She came on to me, Laurie. I'm telling you."

There was no response.

"You don't believe me?"

"Erin's been through a lot. You might be misreading the situation. I'm sure her hugging you is innocent enough."

Will let his head drop. He tried another tack. "What happened to your concern about getting me involved?"

Laurie didn't answer at first. "I just think it would be a good idea to have someone she already knew to talk with." She paused. "But you can do what you want."

Sure he could.

And when the school psychologist got involved and supported Laurie's thinking, he had little room to protest without losing points by sounding insensitive, so he reluctantly took Erin on.

As Will suspected, Erin was high maintenance from the

start. It seemed every time he turned around, she was by his side wanting something. Would he help with her math? She'd had a fight with Kendra. Could she stop by and talk about it?

Will hadn't told anyone except Laurie about Erin's behavior toward him in the woods, and he had to admit there hadn't been a recurrence, which made him think, at times, that Laurie had been right about his misinterpreting Erin's motivation, that she was just upset and needed a fatherly hug. But her comment about his logging chaps nagged at him. He knew he wasn't the most perceptive social animal, but he did think he could tell when someone was hitting on him.

———

On Thursday after classes, Will was in the shop of the forestry shed sharpening the teeth of his chain saw with a file. He loved his Husqvarna. It was ten years old and had seen him through a lot of cuts, proving that if you took good care of something, it would last a long time. Too bad human relationships weren't that easy, he mused.

He heard Erin calling his name from the next room, and he let his head drop in exasperation. He scraped harder, trying to quell his anger over the intrusion. He wasn't even safe from her in his own space. At first he thought there might be a chance that she hadn't heard him, but then the door slowly opened.

"Mr. Buchanan?"

Will looked up. "Yes, Erin. Come in."

"Is this a bad time?"

"No." He picked up the saw. "I'm on my way out, though."

She folded her arms and smiled at him. "I bet you are." She rubbed her elbows as if she were cold. "You've been avoiding me," she said. Her tone was playful, coquettish.

"Not likely," he said. He made his way to the door, but she blocked it. "Let me by, Erin."

She slowly stepped aside, and Will brushed past her. She followed him into the next room. "Can I see you tonight?" she said.

"What about?" He placed the chain saw on the floor.

"I have stuff I need to discuss."

"Like what?" he insisted.

"Well, it's kind of personal."

"Come on, Erin. Stop playing games."

She stepped closer. "I never play games."

For the first time since she'd arrived at the shed, Will had a close-up look at her, and he sensed something wrong. Her eyes were red-rimmed. He could smell alcohol.

"Have you been drinking?"

She put her hand to her mouth and giggled.

"For God's sake, Erin."

"Oh, don't be an old stick-in-the-mud. I was just having a little fun."

"You need to go to the health center."

She touched his hand and played with his middle finger. "You're not going to narc on me, are you?"

He pulled his hand away. "Erin, please."

"You like me. I know you do."

"Why are you doing this?"

"Doing what?"

"You *know* what."

"I want you to say it. Doing what?"

"You need to sleep this off."

She grinned. "Good idea. Can we go to your house?" She

suddenly threw her arms around his neck, and before Will had a chance to break it off, the front door opened.

Kendra stuck her head in. "I'm looking for Erin, is she— Oh, I'm sorry."

———

Kendra left before Will could catch up to her. He immediately shepherded Erin to the health center and got on the phone to the school psychologist, Helen Morgenstern. "I need to talk with you as soon as possible," he said.

"What's going on?"

Will told her only that he was having trouble with a student and that it was urgent.

"Well, my son just got home from school," Helen said. "I have to take care of him first. But I can get away in about an hour. Say four-thirty?"

Will agreed to meet her in her office. The hour to kill felt like a few days. He put in a call to Laurie, but, according to her deputy, Ray, she was out checking into a domestic disturbance. Will felt like telling him he had another one waiting for her when she got back. Instead he asked Ray to relay the message that he'd called and needed to talk with her.

Whatever was motivating Erin right now, Will knew it was beyond his understanding. Despite her seeming adjustment back into school life, she was obviously hurting underneath. But why was she coming on to him? He knew he had to be up-front with Helen about this. Kendra couldn't have walked in at a more inopportune time, and he could just imagine what she'd been thinking. In hindsight he was glad he hadn't been able to catch up with her. What could he possibly have said that would make her believe he was innocent of any prurient behavior with one of his students?

Will headed for Helen's office with a good half-hour lead time. He waited for her, sitting on his hands on a bench outside her door.

When she arrived, she made a show of rattling a fistful of keys to get the right one to fit the office door. Will distrusted people with fat key rings. No one should be that busy or have that much responsibility. He followed her in.

Helen immediately reached for the thermostat. She was a divorced thirty-something, thin, with unnaturally blond hair. She had been close to death once due to complications involving anorexia but had since recovered. Will thought she still looked too thin.

Will felt the heat blasting out through the wall heater.

Helen rubbed her arms. "Phew. Winter is here," she said.

Will wanted to tell her it wasn't cold at all, but he knew that her metabolism probably called for the temperature to be set higher than normal. He nodded and removed his jacket.

"So you caught our friend drinking," Helen said. She motioned for Will to sit in one of the comfy chairs in a corner of the room. She assumed a seat opposite.

Our friend? Will hated that kind of chummy talk. "Well, not really. Not in the act. I smelled alcohol on her."

"So that's one strike already. Just a few weeks into the term."

The strike system at Saxton Mills was sometimes referred to by the students as "the old ball game." Three strikes in an academic year and you're out, never to return. "I guess she won't want me as an adviser anymore," Will said hopefully.

Helen sent him a puzzled look. "Why do you say that?"

"Because I turned her in."

Helen leaned back in her chair and interlaced her bony

fingers. "I think you might be surprised. She thinks an awful lot of you."

"Too much."

"What do you mean?"

Will told Helen about Erin's coming on to him.

"And you're sure about this?"

Will suddenly felt like *he* was the one seeking counseling, and he shifted in his seat. What did she mean, was he sure? Shouldn't he be able to tell? "Yes, I'm sure. I just wanted you to know. Wanted someone to know."

"Well, if what you say is true, it's important that it's out in the open."

"But why is Erin doing this?"

Helen paused and looked up to the ceiling, as if the answer lay somewhere in the tiles. She brought her gaze back to Will. "She probably sees you as the one stable individual in her life now."

"What about Laurie? She's been a rock for her."

"A stable *male* individual."

"Okay. But it still doesn't explain why she's flirting with me."

"It's obviously a confused sexual thing."

"Obviously."

"She probably associates you with finding Josh's body and sees you as the one who was there to give her comfort."

"So?"

"So she likes you."

"But sexually?"

Helen cocked her head to one side. "It's not that unusual, Mr. Buchanan. Teenage girls are always falling in love with their teachers."

"But I'm almost fifty years old."

"Age doesn't matter, Mr. Buchanan."

"What do you mean, it doesn't matter? The law would probably differ with you."

Helen smiled. "What I mean is, these young girls often see one of their teachers as a strong male figure, and they're attracted to him." She paused and looked him in the eyes, still smiling. "Especially one as ruggedly handsome as you."

Will felt his face burn and looked down at the floor. He couldn't think of anything to say.

"I'm sorry, Will. I didn't mean to make you feel uncomfortable," she said. "You've still got a full head of hair, you look like you work out, and you have the energy of a man half your age. You have to admit you wear your years well."

"Gee, thanks, Helen," he said. "But I also know I'm not your typical teenage hunk material." He didn't like where this conversation was leading. It almost began to sound as if it were his fault for being attractive to Erin. "I also know that most teenage girls don't follow through with their fantasies. And that when they do, there's usually something wrong."

"You're absolutely right. As we said at the start, her feelings are confused. She probably also sees you as a father figure."

"Now, *that* I can understand."

"And with her background, not having grown up with her real father, she's finally found him."

Will paused. "I can't believe it."

"What's the matter?"

"I'm nobody's father."

She smiled at him again. "You just need to continue what you're doing. Be firm with her. She'll respond."

"Continue what I'm doing? Isn't that a little dangerous?"

"Dangerous?"

"I'm not talking about Erin. I'm talking about dangerous to me and my career."

"Are you saying you're worried about giving in to her advances?"

"What? God, I'm not saying that!" The suggestion sparked his anger. He slowed his voice down, each word deliberate. "This is a private school, Helen. It's full of kids and faculty who like to talk. Tongue wagging isn't just a pastime—it's a way of life."

"I understand what you're saying, but I think that right now Erin needs you to continue working with her. She's gone through quite a bit of trauma already."

"I just don't want to get caught up in something I can't control."

"I understand. And you were right to talk with me. You shouldn't feel alone in this."

"I just can't seem to make people believe this is really happening."

"I believe you. In fact, I would like to suggest that we get together soon—you, Erin, and me—to discuss your concerns."

"Sounds like a great idea."

"I want to help."

Will got up to leave. He headed for the door, then abruptly turned back. "Can I ask you a question?" he said.

"Sure."

"You keep saying you understand, but I wonder how much you really know about Erin."

"How much do I know about Erin?"

"No disrespect, but I just don't see the science. How can you figure out what the hell she's thinking?"

Chapter 8

ON SATURDAY NIGHT ERIN MISSED IN-DORM CHECK. She hadn't signed out and didn't show up until just before one o'clock on Sunday morning. Her dorm parents had gone through the necessary protocols, informing the administrator on duty, who, in turn, got hold of Headmaster Perry Knowlton. Will found out about this at the Sunday-morning brunch. Perry, knowing Will's habits of taking advantage of school meals, had come into the cafeteria especially to look for him.

"She say anything about where she was?" Will asked, tray in hand.

"She's not talking. I was hoping maybe you could have a chat with her before I do."

"Sure." Will put his tray back in the rack.

"Not now. Please, eat your brunch. She's still sleeping anyway."

"I don't know about this kid, Perry. I think she might be more than we can handle."

Perry led Will over to a corner table. "What can you tell me about her?"

"I know as much as you do. Very little."

Perry looked surprised at Will's response. "I thought maybe you had the inside track. You know, Erin being Laurie's niece and all."

"I never really talked to the kid until a few weeks ago. Laurie didn't discuss her much before that." Will lowered his voice. "You know, Laurie moved out a couple of months ago."

"I heard." He put his hand on Will's shoulder. "You doing okay?"

"Yeah. Things are getting better for us, I think."

Perry pulled his hand away. He took the cover off a salt shaker and rapped it on the table to free the stuck granules. "Helen Morgenstern told me about Erin making a pass at you. I'm glad you said something. "

"That's all I need, right?"

"Try not to be alone with her too much. When you talk with her, make sure other people are around."

At first Will was taken aback by Perry's warning. After all, he had done nothing wrong. But then he remembered that last year Perry had gone through the painful dismissal of a young teacher, a men's soccer coach who'd grown too fond of one of his boys.

"Perhaps you should go along with me," Will said.

"No. I think she might be more likely to open up to you if you were by yourselves."

Will hesitated. "Wait a minute. I'm supposed to be alone with her, but there should be someone there?"

"You know what I mean, Will. Leave the door open, make sure people see you together, that kind of thing."

"This stinks, Perry. We shouldn't have to be this careful."

Perry sighed. "These days you *do* have to be. I don't want another lawsuit right now."

"Lawsuit? Why would there be a lawsuit?"

"If this keeps up, and we follow our dismissal policy, Erin's on her way out of school. Two strikes in a week."

"We could get sued over dismissing her?"

Perry cocked his head. "We could get sued over anything. Where have you been?"

Perry's shoulders lowered, as if the weight of litigious concerns were physical and resting directly on them. At times like this, Will was reminded of why he was not an administrator. He much preferred the blissful ignorance of the classroom.

"So first we kill all the lawyers?" he said.

"Might be a good place to start."

"I think first Erin needs a new adviser."

"Maybe so, but right now you're the man."

"Anything special you want me to say to her?"

"See if you can find out where she was Saturday night. When she came in, her clothes were messed up."

"Does Laurie know about this yet?"

"Of course."

"And . . . ?"

"She agreed that it would be best if the school handled it for now."

"Meaning me."

"Meaning you."

———

It was a brisk fall Sunday afternoon. The foliage was beginning to peak, the large sugar maple in the center of campus especially brilliant in yellow. Heeding Perry's words about not being alone with Erin, he convinced her that a walk in the fresh air would do her some good.

He led Erin across the street and stopped in full view of some students playing an Ultimate Frisbee game on the athletic field that bordered the headmaster's house. He put one foot on the bottom rail of the white fence that ringed the field and leaned his elbows on the top. "I'm trying to understand why you can't tell me where you were last night," Will said for openers.

"I was just out."

"You expect me to believe that you had no reason to be so late?"

Erin seemed drawn and tired, and Will sensed it was not all from lack of sleep. She was on edge, as if she was exhausted from having to keep things inside. "It was a personal thing. I really can't tell you," she said.

"I'm your adviser, Erin, and your friend. How can I help you if you won't open up to me?"

She stared off across the playing field. "I guess there are just some things I can't talk about."

"Is it because you're mad at me?" Will asked.

"Mad at you for what?"

"You know for what."

"For turning me in for drinking?"

"Well, are you?"

She dismissed it with a wave of her hand. "I deserved it. I was stupid."

Her accepting attitude surprised him, and he didn't know what to say. He watched the Frisbee dance through the air, its flight erratic and unpredictable in the wind. One player dove and made an impressive catch.

"I wish I could tell you everything," Erin said. "I know you want to help."

"Were you out with someone?"

"Yes."

"Who?"

"I can't tell you."

"Was it another student?"

She looked away from Will. "Please don't ask me again. I really can't say."

He put his hand on her arm and urged her back toward him. "Are you frightened of something, Erin?"

For a moment Will thought she was going to cry, but she

caught herself. She stood up straight. "There's nothing you can do to help me. There's nothing anyone can do."

"Who is it, Erin?"

"It's a long story. I need to handle it myself."

It was Will's turn to look away. "Fine."

"Please don't be mad at me, Mr. Buchanan."

Will still didn't look at her. "I don't think you know how much trouble you're in," he said.

"You mean with the school?"

"Of course with the school. You've got two strikes now. And that happened in less than a week." He paused. "Do you want to get kicked out of here, Erin?"

"Of course not."

"You're certainly not making noises like you want to stay."

"I'll be good."

"Well, you'll have to be good on your own."

"What do you mean?"

"It means that I'm not going to be your adviser anymore. I can't work with anyone who isn't honest with me."

Will hadn't planned beforehand to abdicate his role as adviser, but it was clear from their conversation that she was not going to open up to him or to anyone else. While he did have second thoughts about his decision, they were fleeting.

Erin took his rejection hard. She showed up at the health center on Monday morning, but they let her go because she wasn't ill. She wandered the campus and skipped all her morning classes. With the absence points accumulated, it would be enough for a third strike and her dismissal from school.

Will didn't find out about this until his afternoon class. He had set up a lab, and he noticed that two of the lab partners had gone missing: Kendra and Sharon Frankle. Kendra was a sharp student, and Will had paired them because he felt they were a good balance of ability and need.

Will went looking for them, became aware of voices coming from the vestibule, and was about to open the door when he heard his name mentioned. He stopped and listened, his hand on the door.

"Where did they find Erin?" It was Sharon's voice.

"Hitchhiking."

"Where was she going?"

"I guess she was babbling something about Mr. Buchanan's house."

Will felt a surge of adrenaline. My God. Erin must be going nuts.

"It was mean for Mr. Buchanan to ditch her," Sharon said.

"She told me he just came right out and said he didn't want to be her adviser."

"I still can't believe they're lovers. Are you really sure?"

"You should hear Erin talk about him. It's sick."

"I don't know," Sharon said. "Mr. Buchanan's kind of cute."

"Come on, Sharon. He's a teacher."

"So?"

"So? What do you mean, 'so'?"

"What's wrong with liking older men?"

"But he's really old."

"If he came on to me, I'd let him."

"You wouldn't."

"Would too."

Sharon lowered her voice further. "You really caught Mr. Buchanan and Erin kissing?"

"I did," Kendra said.

"Really?"

"Really."

"You know, I bet it was getting too hot for them both," Kendra said.

"Too hot for them?"

"People started talking, you know. The administration probably broke them up."

Will had had enough. He pushed open the door. "You two need to get started on the lab," he said.

———

Will struggled to stay focused in class. If Kendra and Sharon were talking about him, he was sure others on the campus were as well. He had to figure out a way to short-circuit this before it got worse. When the class finally ended, he asked Kendra if she wouldn't mind staying after.

"I'm going to be up-front with you, Kendra," he said, his hands clasped behind him, a shoulder against the whiteboard. "I overheard you talking about me before class."

Kendra lowered her head. "I thought you did. I'm sorry."

"Are you really?"

She bit her lower lip but didn't say anything. She was about to cry, and Will realized he would get nowhere if he came on too strong. "Look, let me start again. I'm not interested in getting you into trouble," he said.

"Please. I didn't mean anything by it."

"But you have to understand that what you say can hurt people." Will took a seat next to hers.

"I know. I'm really bad about gossiping."

"Especially if what you're saying isn't true?"

She looked across at him, her eyes moist. "It isn't?"

Will rested his hands on the desk part of the molded plastic chair. "Kendra. Tell me what you think you walked in on the other day."

Kendra paused. "I saw you and Erin hugging."

"And do you know why?"

She colored. "Yes."

"I want you to tell me why you think Erin and I were hugging. I want to hear it from you."

"Because you and Erin are in love."

It took Will a moment to recover from hearing her actually say this.

"It's all she talks about," Kendra added.

"Erin talks about our being in love?"

"All the time."

It was worse than he thought. How could he possibly combat this rumormongering?

"Of course, I didn't believe her at first. She likes to babble on, you know. Sometimes it's hard to sleep."

"But you were convinced when you saw us together."

"Well, yeah. From the way she talked about it after."

Will tried to think of what to say next. If he denied it, Kendra would only think that he was trying to escape responsibility. Yet he had to convince her she was wrong.

"Mr. Buchanan, can I go now? I have soccer practice."

"In a minute, Kendra. I'll give you a pass, don't worry about it."

"My coach doesn't like it if I'm late."

Will pressed on. "Does Erin gossip about our being in love to other people?"

"I don't know. We just talk a lot because we're roommates."

"What exactly does she say about me?"

"Oh, that you're strong and always there for her. That you're good . . ." She hesitated.

"That I'm good?"

"That you're good in bed, all right?"

Will let his chin drop to his chest. "Oh, God."

"Well, that's what she said." Kendra folded her arms. "I really need to go."

"Did she talk about where she was the other night?"

"Yeah. She said she was out with you."

Will raised his head and met her eyes. "That's not true, Kendra. And I can prove it."

She shrugged her shoulders. "Okay."

"I was out with someone else that night. Erin's been lying to you all along."

"I'm just telling you what she said." She bit her lower lip again.

"Look, Kendra"—he lowered his voice—"this is serious. You can imagine how devastating this would be if people believed I was having an affair with a student."

"I know." It was too much. Kendra broke down.

Will gave her his handkerchief. "I'm not asking you to believe me right now, but I am asking that you not talk about this alleged affair anymore."

She sniffled. "I won't. I'm sorry."

"You have to know that I'm worried about Erin. I think she's really in trouble."

"Yeah. She's really getting weird. She stays up most of the night."

"Doing what?"

"Mostly writing stuff on her computer."

"What do you mean, 'stuff'?"

"I don't know. She won't let anyone see it." She blew her nose. "I tried to sneak a peek once when she was out of the room. She caught me and said she was going to kill me if I did it again."

"She said that? She was going to kill you?"

"Yeah. And she didn't look like she was kidding around."

"She really threatened you?"

"Well, she had that look in her eye. Like the one she gets late at night staring at the screen." She held out the handkerchief to Will, but he gestured for her to keep it. "It's scary," she continued. "You wouldn't believe how fast her fingers move. And she talks to herself."

"What does she say?"

"I'm not sure. She repeats the same thing over and over."

"What?"

"It's something like 'Caballa' or 'Willhalla,' or something like that. I couldn't quite understand."

Will thought a moment. "You sure you can't remember exactly what she said?"

"No. And I don't want to."

"Why not?"

"It freaked me out, Mr. Buchanan," Kendra said.

"It must have," Will said.

———

Will called Laurie that evening to make sure she was informed of all that had happened. She wasn't too happy about his decision to quit being Erin's adviser, and he tried to convince her he'd been on a dead-end road.

"But she's so fragile now," she said. "This might push her over the edge."

"Maybe so. But I just can't work with her anymore." He told her about Erin's bizarre fantasy of their having an affair. There was a pause on the line. "You're serious, aren't you."

"Damn straight."

Laurie was silent.

Will took a breath. "Look. I know this is hard to hear, but if this keeps up, the whole school is going to think I'm having an affair with Erin."

"What can I do?"

"I don't know. Talk to her? Convince her I'm not her lover?"

"I'll try, but I don't know how much she'll listen."

"I thought you two were best buddies."

"She's been ignoring me lately."

"I think she's seeing someone," Will said. "I'm convinced that's where she was on Saturday night."

"Any idea who?"

"No. And I don't want to think about it."

"I'm sorry you're giving up on her."

"I'm not giving up. I just don't want to be her adviser anymore. It doesn't help her, and it's too risky for me."

"You *are* giving up."

"Come on, Laurie. That isn't fair."

"Fine. I'll talk to you later."

The line went dead. Will stared at the phone for a moment, then placed it on the cradle.

Perry decided to dismiss the absence points for the missed classes on Monday because of Erin's emotional state, but she was placed on a short tether. The next infraction would probably be her last. Will went about his business the rest of the week. He stayed away from Erin and kept to himself.

But he couldn't stop thinking about how Kendra had described Erin as spending her nights in front of the computer in a state of some sort of mystical logorrhea. He bet that if he could get hold of what she'd written, it might reveal the identity of the person she'd been out with on Saturday night. Erin spelled trouble for him, but he couldn't stop wanting to help her.

And there was the Laurie piece of the puzzle, too. How had he somehow managed to mess things up with her again? All week long he fought the urge to call her back, stubbornly thinking that the next move was hers. It was she who'd hung up on him, after all. Besides, he was right about resigning his responsibilities with Erin. He knew it in his gut.

On Thursday night Will was at home, about to pour himself a Laphraoig, when he heard a knock at the door. It was Erin.

"I'm sorry to bother you," she said. "Can I come in?"

Will stood with his hand on the door. He felt like closing it in her face, but then he had a good look at her cheek. There was a bruise under her eye. "Are you okay?" he asked.

She managed a smile. "I'm fine." But she wasn't fine, and she began to whimper.

Like a man poised on a high wire, Will took a careful step toward her. It was enough of an invitation for her to reach out, and he found himself, his arms awkwardly outstretched, letting her hug him again.

"I just need to feel safe for a few minutes. I won't stay long," she whispered in his ear.

Will pulled away from her. "Who did this to you, Erin? Who hit you?"

"It doesn't matter."

"I'm going to call Laurie." He turned, but Erin grabbed his arm.

"No. Please. No cops."

"Cops? Erin, Laurie's also your aunt."

"It doesn't matter." She tried to pull herself together. "I shouldn't have come here."

Will walked into the living room and reached for the phone. She followed and grabbed his arm again. "You'll just make it worse," she said.

Will studied her for a moment. "What can I do to help, then?"

"Nothing. I only came by to say I was sorry. I didn't mean to hurt you."

"You didn't. At least not yet."

"I was being silly telling Kendra you and I were lovers."

"I know."

"It was nice to think about, though."

"Tell me who hurt you, Erin."

"I'm going to leave now, " she said. "I just wanted to say I was sorry about everything."

Will reached to stop her, but she slapped his hand away. "Don't touch me."

The change in her was so abrupt that Will stepped back as if he'd accidentally awakened a sleeping mad dog.

"You could have had me," she said. "You had your chance."

———

After Erin left, Will called the station, but Laurie was out on her rounds. He left a message with Ray that Laurie should be on the lookout for Erin. Then he put the phone down and stared at it. He couldn't get Erin's bruised and swollen face out of his mind, and for the first time he felt he had some glimmer of understanding of what was going on with her. He jumped in his car, driving the streets, but there was no sign of her, so finally he headed to Perry's house. He knew that the headmaster would be in because he had just returned from a two-day fund-raising trip to Boston and, under the circumstances, would want to know right away what was happening with Erin.

The headmaster's residence, an updated two-story Federal, was originally the main farmhouse of the old estate that eventually became Saxton Mills School. Perry had furnished it with period pieces; a heavy armoire, a nicely detailed harpsichord, and a Queen Anne writing desk were among Will's favorites. Will was greeted at the door and ushered into the living room. Perry poked at the ashes in the fireplace and put on another log.

"You say her face was bruised?"

"She looked terrible, Perry."

"And you have no idea where she went after she left your house?"

"No. It happened so fast. Then I drove around looking for her." Will could feel his heart racing. "I checked with her dorm before I came to your place, but no one's seen her since this afternoon." He paused. "I feel terrible about this, Perry. I just didn't see it. It never occurred to me that she was in an abusive relationship."

"Take it easy, Will." Perry placed the poker back on the hearth. "There's no need to blame yourself."

"You should have seen her. She looked awful . . . so sad, so hurt."

Perry put a hand on Will's shoulder. "Why don't you sit down, Will. Let's talk this out."

"I don't want to sit down. I need to find that kid."

"Does Laurie know about this yet?"

"I left a message." Will zipped up his jacket. "I'm going back out to look for her. I just wanted to let you know what's going on."

Will left Perry to do a more thorough search of the campus while he drove around looking for Laurie's cruiser. He made several trips along the backroads but there was still no sign of her. He kept wondering who Erin was seeing and couldn't help thinking of the voice on the phone and the dark figure he'd seen at Zealand Falls. He drove back and forth through town, but finally gave up a little after midnight.

When he pulled into his driveway, he was surprised to find the cruiser waiting for him. Deputy Ray Flemmer got out and approached the truck. He shone his flashlight at Will.

"Where's Laurie?" Will asked, shielding his eyes.

"Busy."

"What's going on?"

"Get out of the truck, please," Flemmer said.

"Sure, Ray."

When Will opened the door, Flemmer grabbed him by the arms and spun him around. "Hands on the truck," he said. He patted Will down. "Sorry. I have to place you under arrest." He reached for his cuffs.

Will turned around and held out his hands. "This is ridiculous, Ray. What's the charge?"

"Felonious sexual assault." Flemmer read him his rights.

Chapter 9

WILL WAS FAMILIAR WITH THE SMALL HOLDING CELL at the police station. He'd been locked up in it three years before when he was falsely accused of murdering one of his students. It had been painted since, the sagging bunks rebuilt.

"I like what you've done to the place," Will said to Laurie as she opened the cell door. "Not as drab."

"I don't know how you can be so cavalier about this," she said.

Will sat on a bunk, and she took a seat on the one across from him. "You don't expect me to take this seriously." She left the cell door open, with Flemmer standing guard.

"Erin fingered you, Will."

Will smiled. "Poor choice of words."

Laurie shook her head and got up to leave.

"No, don't go. I'll be good."

She resumed her seat and glanced at Flemmer. "Give us a minute, okay?"

After Flemmer left, Will said, "Great. Now that he's gone, we can make our break."

"For God's sake, Will. Can you be serious for one minute?"

"I'm just nervous, that's all. I didn't do anything wrong."

"I'll start again. Erin says you raped her."

"Well, Erin is deranged."

"She's in the hospital, Will. Pretty beat up."

"When was I supposed to have done this?"

"At your house, earlier in the evening."

"She's lying."

Laurie leaned forward, arms on her knees, her hands clasped together. Will thought for a moment she was going to ask for him to pray along with her. "Look, Will, I don't believe for one minute that you did this to her. I'm just trying to find out what she said to you. Now, it's true, isn't it, that she was at your house last night?"

Will didn't hesitate. "Yes, she was at our house last night."

Laurie rolled her hand as a sign for him to keep talking.

"She came to the house about seven," Will said, then paused.

"Come on, Will. I'm not going to keep prompting you. Tell me everything that happened."

Will recounted all that he could remember, including Erin's turning on him as her final gesture. "It was frightening to watch her change so quickly."

"And you're sure you saw a bruise under her eye."

"It was more than that. Her face was all puffy."

Laurie studied his eyes a moment, then looked away.

"You don't believe me."

"Of course I believe you," she said.

"Then why did you turn away?"

"I don't know. Maybe I just didn't want to hear any more. This is upsetting."

"If I raped her, why would I go to see Perry and report it? Why would I spend half the night looking for her?"

"I said I believe you, Will. Stop protesting so much." Laurie got up from her seat, leaned up against the bars, and stared out into the corridor.

"Someone's put her up to this," Will continued.

Laurie didn't turn around. "Yes, that appears to be the case."

"Either that or she's making the whole thing up."

She wheeled back to him. "Come on, Will. It wasn't a phantom rapist."

"So we're left with someone threatening her. You know, if she tells the truth, she'll really get beat up."

Laurie folded her arms and thought a moment. "But why the setup? Why you? That's what I don't get."

"Because I'm there? I don't know. Either it's that or it's really personal and someone's out to get me."

"You think that's the case?"

Will stared at her a moment, then shook his head. "I don't know. I just don't know."

Laurie gazed up at the ceiling. "What's happened to her?" she said. "It's almost as if she's become another person since Josh's death."

Will stood. "I'm tired of talking about Erin. I mean, I'm sorry and everything, and probably being insensitive, but what the hell am I going to do?"

"You need a lawyer."

"So this is really going to stick? I can't believe it."

"Right now it's Erin's word against yours. I'm sure I'll find out more when I finally get a chance to talk to her."

"You haven't seen her yet?"

"She called the rape crisis center in Conway, and they brought her right to the hospital. There's a protocol they follow from then on."

"Well, she knew right where to call, didn't she."

"What's that supposed to mean?"

"It means this was all planned," he said. "So let me guess. They won't let you see her, right?"

"No. It's not that. They just need to do some things first."

"Like what?"

"They'll use a rape kit on her, you know, a vaginal swipe and scrape of skin for hair and fiber evidence."

"I see."

"And eventually DNA testing."

Will sat forward. "Of course. And that should prove I didn't do it."

"Yes. I think so."

"What do you mean, you *think* so? I didn't do it, remember?" For the first time since he'd been put in the cell, he felt he might have a chance. "Then I should be out of here in no time."

"It takes over a month to get the lab results."

"Great. What happens to me in the meantime?"

Laurie considered. "You know, maybe you should get Malvina Lincoln as your lawyer. I bet she'd jump at the chance."

"Who?"

"I've talked to you about her before. She's from Concord."

"Isn't she that raging feminist who's out to castrate any male she sees?"

"Well, I wouldn't characterize her quite that way."

———

Malvina Lincoln drove up to Saxton Mills from Concord after lunch. Will didn't expect to see her so soon, if at all. He couldn't figure out why she'd be interested in the accused when her track record had always been with the victim, but Laurie explained that Malvina had had her stint as a state's attorney and now was in private practice. Laurie had a hunch it just might be a good match, and who was he to argue? It's not like he had options.

Laurie opened the cell door, and Malvina strode in casually, as if it were her living room. "All right," she said. "Let's hear what you have to say."

Will had spent the morning trying to sleep. He was exhausted, and her entrance jolted him upright. "How's 'Pleased to meet you' for starters?" he said.

Malvina ignored him. She was a statuesque black woman who wore her hair in cornrows decorated with white beads. She commanded attention by her stiff carriage and dark eyes. She took out a legal pad and a pencil from her black leather briefcase. "I know who you are, Will, and you know who I am. Let's not waste time."

The first thing Will noticed as she sat on the other bunk and crossed her legs was her muscular calves. He could just imagine what would happen if he commented on them, and he wondered why his reaction to stress seemed to bring out his impish side. Perhaps gallows humor was the only defense he had left. He tried to focus but felt sick from lack of sleep. "I'm innocent," he said.

"We all are." She adjusted her skirt. "This is a serious charge, Will. I'm going to be up-front with you."

"I know it's serious."

"I'm sure on some level you do. But especially in cases like this, when the victim points the finger, we're going to be hard-pressed to defend you."

Will studied her. "Is that supposed to encourage me?"

"I just want you to know what you're up against. Rape is a hot-button issue. There's a lot of political pressure to convict."

"So I'm dead meat. Is that what you're telling me?"

"I just want to prepare you that this might be tougher than you think."

Will was trying to keep his head straight, but he was still groggy from lack of sleep. "But I'm innocent," was all he managed to repeat.

"Sometimes even the innocent have little defense."

"What?"

"Think about it, Will. A young girl shows up at a rape crisis center. It's clear that she's been beaten up. I mean, someone's really done a number on her. She says she was raped and identifies the one who did it. The guy gets arrested and says he didn't do it. Who are you going to believe?"

She wagged her pencil as she talked, and Will couldn't take his eyes off it.

"Will?"

"Yeah. I heard you."

"And the prosecution doesn't have to prove 'beyond a reasonable doubt' either, to make a case against you."

"So if it just looks like I'm guilty, then that's okay, is that what you're saying?"

"The phrase is called 'more likely than not.' "

"As in the phrase 'it is more likely than not that Will Buchanan raped Erin Wickham.' "

"Given the preponderance of evidence, of course."

"What a crock." Will thought a moment. "What about DNA?"

"If the DNA's not yours, not tainted in any way, it should absolve you."

" 'More likely than not.' "

Malvina paused. "Regardless of what happens, you're looking at jail time until this sorts itself out if you can't make bail." She recrossed her legs. "I want you to tell me all you can about Erin Wickham. I want to know what she said, where she said it, what you said in return, and—most important—who can corroborate it."

Will looked out into the corridor. He hadn't noticed that Laurie had left but surmised it was probably in deference to attorney-client privilege. It was true—he'd been arrested, he was in jail. He repeated it to himself like a mantra to make it sink in and help him concentrate.

"And only then," Malvina continued, "will I make up my mind whether I'll take this case."

Will talked for two hours. Malvina scrawled all over the lines, filling up pages of the yellow pad. She didn't edit or interrupt him.

"I can't think of anything else right now," Will said.

"You did a good job, Will."

"Does that mean you're going to represent me?"

"I'll let you know tomorrow. After I do some poking around."

"I guess that means you're going to the school to ask questions."

"That's right."

Will let his head drop. "Wonderful."

"Don't worry. I'll be politic and deferential."

"Sure. You do that."

"Listen. You're in a lot of trouble, but you've got to keep your spirits up. I can't promise anything, but if I don't find you've been lying to me, I'll probably take the case."

"Why?"

"Why? Because you need help."

"But why come to my defense, Malvina? Don't you like to hang guys like me by the balls?"

Malvina stared hard at Will.

Will didn't look away. "I'm sorry. I have to ask you this. I know your reputation."

"You mean as a ball buster?"

"For lack of a better expression, yes."

"I don't know. Maybe it's *because* of my reputation I'm interested in the case." She pointed her pencil at him. "I can tell you this: If I take you on, you'll get my full attention. I don't do things half-assed."

"What happens to me next?"

"You'll go before the district court tomorrow for arraignment and a bail hearing. I'm going to try to have you released on your own recognizance. No bail."

"I don't have much money."

"Don't worry about it now."

"So then what happens?"

"A probable-cause hearing date is set. If you have to come up with bail, then I can argue for bail plus corporate surety, which primarily means it doesn't have to be all cash. But that usually involves a bail bondsman, and I don't know if the judge will go along with it."

"Sounds complicated."

"It's what lawyers do."

"Like a game of 'gotcha.'"

"More like save your ass."

"My ass is in your hands, Malvina."

Will finally got a smile out of her. Malvina put her pad and pencil back in her briefcase. "I'll see you tomorrow, I guess."

"Suppose I can't make bail, Malvina?"

She held the briefcase in both hands across her middle. "Then you'll be placed in the county jail until your probable-cause hearing."

"And how long does it take to get one of those?"

"By law, it has to be within ten days."

"Ten days in the slammer!"

It sounded real funny when he said it, and he almost laughed. Almost.

Chapter 10

THE NORTHERN CARROLL COUNTY COURTHOUSE IN Conway, New Hampshire, has a long roof and a tower at one end. Recently constructed, with a handy companion police building that runs perpendicular, it sits lengthwise along a large parking lot. The architecture made Will think, as Laurie turned the cruiser into the driveway, of a modern country church whose congregation had run out of money before they could construct a steeple.

The ride up from Saxton Mills, Malvina sharing the front seat with Laurie, did little to calm his nerves. As many times as he'd been in Laurie's cruiser, he had never sat in the back, and, staring through the protective grille with the barrel of her shotgun poised between the front seats in his line of vision, he truly felt the criminal.

Laurie parked the cruiser. She opened the back door, and Will jerked his butt across the seat. The handcuffs bit his wrists as he moved. He stepped out onto the pavement. It was nice to feel the sun on his face. It had been only a day and a half, but it had seemed an eternity since he'd been outside. Just this moment in the sun was a delicious taste of freedom. It made him ache for more, but Laurie took him by the arm, and soon he was inside the courthouse.

To Will's surprise, Perry Knowlton was waiting for him in the lobby. Perry went to shake his hand, and there was an awkward moment as he fumbled with the handcuffs. "I wanted to be here, Will."

"I appreciate it."

Initially Perry acted as if he wanted to continue the conversation, but he seemed to forget what he was going to say.

"I think they're ready for us," Malvina said. "You're first on the docket."

They entered the courtroom through two heavy doors. It didn't look much different from what Will had expected—a judge's bench in front where it should be, and a table each for the prosecution and defense. The American flag and state flag stood on opposite ends of the bench. Malvina nodded to the state's attorney. "Morning, Toby."

Toby Mancuso closed his jacket and stepped forward. "Malvina, it's good to see you." He shook her hand.

Will sat down in the chair Malvina indicated. The bailiff soon asked them to rise, the judge walked in, and the proceedings began.

Judge Murray Walker looked as if he had been born to the bench. He was angular and bald, with more a beak than a nose, and his movements were crisp, with an edge to them that suggested he was always in a hurry. As Malvina had explained to Will, the event shouldn't take long; this procedure was more to decide when to meet again after determining how much of a threat Will was to the outside world.

The state's attorney began the proceedings. After a long speech about the heinous act and the need for society to act swiftly in such cases, Toby finished with, "Your Honor, given the gravity of this crime, the state recommends that bail be set at twenty-five thousand." He sat down.

Will felt a numbness in the back of his neck. The last time he'd even thought in terms of that kind of money was when he'd built the house, and that was when he'd had to borrow it.

"Your Honor," Malvina said, "isn't that a bit excessive?" She gestured toward Will. "My client has never been in trouble with the law. He has been an excellent teacher for many years, truly an outstanding member of the community."

"I understand that, Ms. Lincoln," Judge Walker said, "but I'm sure you also agree with the state that these are serious charges."

"And I'm sure I don't need to remind the court," Malvina said, "that is exactly what they are. Unsubstantiated charges."

Walker smiled at her. "You don't mean that you're going to start arguing this case now, do you, Ms. Lincoln?"

"Certainly not. I'm only trying to emphasize that this is not a man who would do such a thing. He's not a threat to society."

Toby stood up to protest, but Walker waved him down. "You remember, Ms. Lincoln, that your client is accused of a serious felony."

"Yes, sir."

"Well, let's set a date for the hearing, and then you can argue all you want. Given the circumstances, the state's request seems fair."

—————

The state wanted cash only, no corporate surety. Since Will didn't have the ready dough, he was remanded to the Carroll County House of Correction in Ossipee until he could pony up twenty-five grand. If that should happen, Judge Walker had conveniently set bail conditions. Will was to report once a week to a probation officer and not use any alcohol, drugs, or firearms.

The ride to the county jail took less than an hour, the last few miles along a winding country road. The three-story jail, surrounded by fields, was an odd combination of buildings, one made of brick with a same-size white clapboard building attached, the red metal roof rusted in places. At first, when Laurie pulled into the long driveway, Will thought that the buildings closest to the road—elongated, flat-roofed, sixties kitsch—were the jail, and his spirits momentarily lifted. This wouldn't be too bad. It looked like his junior high school. But they soon passed a sign indicating that the buildings belonged to the county home for the elderly.

That you could live out the last of your days within earshot of criminals and dangerous misfits struck Will as laughable, but when the cruiser came to a stop, he felt his stomach clench, and he immediately lost any sense that what he was about to face was going to be humorous.

Malvina turned in the front seat and looked directly at him. "Don't worry, Will," she said. "You won't be staying long. We'll get you out of here soon."

"Plan on robbing a bank?"

"We'll find the money somewhere."

Laurie stepped out of the cruiser and opened the back door. Will again struggled to slide his rump across the seat. Did they really have to handcuff him? Laurie closed the door. Malvina remained in the car. "Good luck," she said.

Laurie took him by the arm, and they walked up the steps together toward the main door. Someone must have seen them through the door window coming in, for as soon as Laurie placed her hand on the door handle, a loud buzzer sounded.

The noise startled Will as it must have Laurie, for her hand jumped off the handle as if it were electrified. She grabbed it again and this time held on as a second, longer buzz freed the lock again.

To the right as they walked in was a windowed office, what Will took to be a guardhouse of sorts, and through the door strode a man with a pronounced paunch.

He shook Laurie's hand. "I'm Captain Keenan McCurtin," he said. "I'm ready to take your prisoner." He immediately grabbed Will by the arm and led him to a room off to the left. "You'll wait in the holding cell," he told Will, "until I'm ready to process you." That said, he closed and locked the door with one of the keys he swiftly chose from a large ring.

It all happened so quickly that at first Will just stood in the center of the room. He could still hear Laurie's voice in the hallway. Then it was quiet.

He sat down on a bunk to wait and stared at the walls, two-tone, with cream color at the top and a light robin's-egg blue running along the bottom. The bars on the cell door were painted chocolate brown.

Laurie had removed his watch, so he didn't know how long he'd been waiting in the holding cell, but he figured it had been over an hour before Captain McCurtin returned.

"Sorry to keep you waiting," McCurtin said, almost amiably. "I had to give the OIC a hand."

"The what?"

"Officer in charge."

"Oh."

"Let's get you processed," he said. With a hand on Will's elbow, McCurtin steered him across the hall to another room. As they walked in, Will's eye was drawn to the left, to several shelves containing paperbacks. "Our little library," McCurtin said.

Will nodded.

"Ever been in jail before?" McCurtin asked.

"No. Well, just overnight."

McCurtin nodded. Will noticed his badge. Part of the blue color surrounding his name was chipped, and if the wear was any indication, McCurtin had been doing this job for a while. "This shouldn't take long," McCurtin said. "I have to finger-print you, take your picture, that sort of thing."

"Okay."

As McCurtin was taking care of the processing, Will kept thinking, as he looked around, that the jail was definitely a low-tech facility. There were no electronic doors whirring and slamming anywhere, and McCurtin's key ring made him appear laughable, a cartoon parody of a jailer.

"How old is this place?" Will asked.

"Dates back to the 1700s."

"You're kidding."

"Nope. Actually, the original cells came from the brig of an old battleship. They were set in place by a crane and the walls built around them."

"Fascinating," Will said, but all he could think about was rats.

McCurtin made him stand with his back to a door with a height chart on it. He took his picture. He let Will pick out his own uniform from a large cardboard box. "Orange. Not blue," McCurtin instructed.

"What's the difference?"

"Orange is pretrial. Blue is for trusties."

"Trusties?" Will smiled.

"That's funny?"

"What are trusties?"

"Convicted inmates. They're doing time."

Will shook his head.

"You still think it's funny?" McCurtin said.

"It's just that with my work 'trustees' are a different sort of animal."

McCurtin looked thoughtfully at Will. "I think you'll find a lot of things different in here."

McCurtin led Will down to Tier C and showed him the cell he would share with three others. His new orange outfit felt stiff at the knees. At first he thought he might ask McCurtin what the HOC stenciled on his back meant, but he didn't want to sound too much like a rookie and thought better of it. When they reached Tier C, Will was surprised to find no one at home.

"They're in the exercise yard," McCurtin explained.

"Where's that?"

"You'll find out soon enough."

Tier C consisted of a unit, or pod, of five cells with a common area, also barred, that ran the length of the cells. Three hours a day, according to McCurtin, prisoners were let out and were free to roam this common area, what he referred to as "the bullpen," where they could make only collect calls from the pay phone or try to watch a dinky black-and-white TV with lousy reception.

McCurtin showed him his bunk. "You're lucky," he said.

"I am?"

"Yeah. You've got a bunk. Manheim's in lockdown."

"What for?"

McCurtin winked at Will. "Manheim screwed up," he said. "That's all you need to know."

"Right."

The lines in McCurtin's hard face tightened. "I wouldn't

ask a lot of questions in here, Buchanan. Don't laugh at something you don't understand. Keep to yourself and you'll be all right."

Keep to himself? With three others in this freezer-carton-size room? Still, it was a gesture that Will sensed McCurtin didn't have to make. "Okay," he said.

Before his cellmates returned, Will made up his bunk. At the end of the cell was a stainless-steel toilet, painted the ubiquitous chocolate brown, with no lid. He stared at it, wondering where the curtain or door had gotten to, when it occurred to him that the HOC stood for "House of Correction." He was glad he hadn't asked McCurtin.

Then he heard the door to Tier C open and voices in the hallway. He stood at the back of the cell and waited as one by one his cellmates entered, a short, bald guy first, then one with a shock of red hair, followed by an over-six footer, heavily muscled, with his sleeves rolled up.

The one with the biceps spoke first. "The new guy," he said. He studied Will like he'd study a used car.

"I'm Nunzio," the bald one said. He pointed to the biceps guy. "This is Smith."

Will nodded.

The mate with the red hair climbed up to the top bunk, rolled onto his back, and stared at the ceiling.

Smith said, "That's Porker." He jerked a thumb to the top bunk. "He's not very friendly."

Will was immediately drawn to Smith. He seemed at ease with himself.

Porker rolled over onto his elbows and said to Will, "You don't call me Porker. You call me 'mister.' "

"Mister!" Nunzio climbed up on the bunk and started pummeling Porker. "How 'bout Mr. Pigfucker. 'Mister,' my ass."

Smith grinned at Will. "Welcome to Club Med," he said.

"Who are you?"

Will told him his name.

"Figured it was you," Smith said.

Porker grabbed Nunzio's arms, and Nunzio grappled him to the floor. He kicked Porker.

"Cut it out," Smith said. Nunzio immediately pulled back. Porker got up and brushed himself off.

The interlude revealed much to Will. Smith was in charge, at least in the cell.

"Just read about you," Smith said. "You're all over the newspaper. You like little girls."

"Christ, not another one," Nunzio said.

Smith said, "Not like Manheim." He paused. "Buchanan here likes them a little older. He's a teacher."

"A teacher!" Porker stepped closer and stared at Will.

Will could smell his sour breath.

"A teacher," he repeated, as if trying to remember exactly what that was.

"I guess you did a number on her," Smith said.

"I didn't touch her."

"Of course you didn't," Smith said.

Will tried to sleep after lights-out, but there was a steady drip coming from somewhere, and he sat up most of the night listening to it. At least he hadn't seen any rats. Yet. He couldn't stop thinking about Manheim and what had happened to him.

Smith had calmly explained that Manheim was a "skinner," a child molester who preyed on his victims using the Internet. Inmates don't like child molesters, the mouth breathers and bottom feeders, the lowest of the low in the social hierarchy of the jail. Manheim had been thrashed pretty good, almost killed, according to Smith. He'd been locked down for his own safety. Will wondered about *his* place in the pecking order. It didn't look good. If the prison population considered a teenage girl a child, he was in trouble.

Will lay thinking about this and the brown stainless-steel toilet without a seat. He knew sooner or later he would have to use it, but it really wasn't an inviting place to drop his pants. When he finally drifted off, the toilet had somehow been transformed into an alien spacecraft with him sitting on top of it, plunger as joystick, rocketing over the backdrop of a Buck Rogers moonscape.

———

Around ten the next morning, Malvina was there to see him. He was let out of his cell and brought to the visitation room. Due to proximity, the room also served as a place where Tier C people took their meals, which were prepared in the state old people's home, warmed up at suppertime, and distributed in compartmented metal trays. The room had heavy wooden benches painted chocolate brown. They must have had a sale on that color paint, and Will was getting sick of looking at it.

True to form, Malvina dispensed with the pleasantries and cut to the chase. "There's been a new development, Will."

"The real rapist confessed?"

"I wish that were the case." She paused. "Erin took off."

"Oh, great."

"She stole a car from one of the volunteers at the rape crisis center."

"You know that for sure? I mean, how do you know she wasn't kidnapped?"

"Well, unless she was forced to write the note she left, she did it all on her own."

"What does the note say?"

"That she was sorry about stealing the car and would take good care of it."

"That's it?"

Malvina nodded.

Will sat back in his chair.

"Any ideas about where she might be?" Malvina asked.

"No, I don't."

"She never mentioned a getaway place to you, some safe haven maybe?"

"Come on, Malvina. I didn't know her that well, remember?"

"Tell me about Kendra McCullen."

"So you've been talking to Kendra."

"She thinks you knew Erin better than you claim."

"Yeah, well Kendra has a fertile imagination."

"Do you have any idea why Erin kept talking to her about your being her lover?"

Will shook his head no, then grew silent.

Malvina said, "Look, Will. I'm only asking you this because the state's attorney is going to do the same thing. It would be nice if I didn't have any surprises."

"I wish I could help you out," he said, "but I don't have a clue." He studied her face for a reaction, but she remained deadpan. "Have you talked to the school psychologist?"

"I have."

"Then you know that she thinks it's a confused sexual thing."

He must have sounded incredulous, for Malvina said, "But you don't agree?"

Will could feel his pulse pounding near his temple. "I think Erin was looking for me to take care of her. There's someone else involved we don't know about, and I think she wanted me to get between the two of them."

"And who is this someone else?"

"Whoever she went to see when she was late for in-dorm time. Whoever made the anonymous phone call."

Malvina wrote on her legal pad. "The same person who raped her?"

"Who else?"

"And so, despite Erin's overtures to you, this really wasn't sexual."

"That's right."

"But why set you up?"

Will fidgeted on the bench. "I've been through this before."

"Humor me."

"Whoever raped her had put her up to scamming me, threatened her, bullied her into doing what he wanted."

"So it's possible someone did force her to write that note about stealing the car."

Both were quiet for a few moments, and then Will said, "I wonder, Malvina, if we know for sure Erin was raped. What did the tests show?"

"Semen in her underwear, for one thing."

"And . . . ?"

Malvina's brow knitted as she appeared to be choosing her words carefully. "Some vaginal bruising."

"Could it have been consensual?"

Malvina thought a moment. "Perhaps."

"So it's even possible that a rape never happened. That Erin made up the whole thing."

"I doubt that, Will. She was badly beaten. Someone did that to her."

"But the DNA from the semen should show once and for all that it wasn't me."

"It should."

"What do you mean, 'It should'?"

Malvina sighed. "It will eventually show conclusively that you didn't do it. But right now we have to focus on getting you out of here." She put her legal pad into her briefcase, a less-than-subtle sign that the conversation was over.

"Thanks for coming," Will said. "It's nice to talk to a civilian."

"How are you holding up?"

He shrugged his shoulders. "I would prefer not to be here."

"Perry thinks he'll be able to come up with the money soon."

"What?"

"Your headmaster."

"I know who Perry is."

"Nice man."

Will leaned closer to the bars. "No. No way that's going to happen."

Malvina hesitated. "I guess I don't understand."

"Perry doesn't have twenty-five grand to give."

"He's called an emergency board meeting. He's sure he can convince them to get you out of here."

"Tell him I appreciate it, but he should forget it."

"You enjoy being in jail that much?"

"Of course not. But the last thing I want to do is put the school in jeopardy. One of our students has accused me of raping her. How would it look if the school backed me and bailed me out?"

"Conflict of interest?"

"Please. Tell him no."

Malvina stood. "I'll tell him."

"I can make it in here until the probable-cause hearing, I know that." Will thought a moment. "Does Erin's disappearance change that at all? I mean, what's going to happen?"

"I don't know. We'll have to see. There might be a continuance until Erin shows up. I imagine the state would like to have her there as a witness."

"Great. Prolong the agony."

"You sure you don't have any money stashed away? Lottery winnings? A rich uncle?"

"Just my retirement."

"Use it."

"No. It's the principle of the thing."

"Principle? What principle?"

Will stared at her. "If you don't know, then you don't know me."

———

Will wasn't sure what the principle was either, but it had something to do with his stubborn pride, with the stern, Yankee assumption that the innocent shouldn't have to buy their freedom. He appreciated Perry's gesture, but he was sure the probable-cause hearing would clear him of all wrongdoing. The date had been set for next Thursday, a mere nine days away, unless the judge decided to move it back because of Erin's disappearance.

In the bullpen, during his three hours of relative freedom, he was allowed to read a newspaper. It was the local Conway weekly that Malvina had left for him, and it carried coverage of the alleged rape and his arrest, but it was too old to include anything about Erin's stealing the car. Where could she have gone? If it was true that she'd stolen it on her own, it meant that whoever had done this to her was probably out tracking her down. She was, no doubt, still in danger even if she had escaped on her own.

What also caught Will's attention was a second-page story on a recent land deal. There was a picture of Laurie's brother shaking hands with Jackson Lloyd IV. The title read: "A New Ski Area?" According to the article, plans were afoot to explore the possibility of developing the land on Hunger Mountain, part of the Lloyd estate near Campton.

The picture was grainy, but it revealed clearly enough both men beaming over the transaction. All the photo needed was dollar signs floating above their heads. At first Will couldn't be certain, because of the bad light and graininess of the photo, but with the help of the light cast by the TV, the photo also revealed that Jackson Lloyd IV was wearing a large watch that looked exactly like the Rolex Will had found in the woods.

The image jumped out at him. Will hadn't thought about the Rolex since his arrest, and the discovery brought to the surface questions that had lain dormant. Did Zippy lie about Josh's not wearing a watch? Who had placed that phone call to his office? Will had no idea about how the Rolexes were tied together, but seeing one on the wrist of the elder Lloyd brother only served to convince him more firmly that the watches were actually part of a larger pattern that involved an explanation of Erin and her strange behavior.

————

Later that evening, after lights-out, Will and Smith had a whispered conversation.

"Your lawyer believe your side of the story?" Smith asked.

"I think so."

"You're lucky, then."

"I take it your lawyer doesn't believe you?"

Smith didn't answer.

Will could make out the shadowed figure of the man as he sat hunched, elbows resting on his knees, on the edge of the bunk.

"Did you rape that kid?" Smith asked after a few moments.

"No."

"That's good."

"You believe me?"

"I believe you can be in this hole without being guilty of anything."

Will mulled over Smith's observation. "So what are you in for?"

"They claim I killed my best friend. Does that make sense to you?"

"No," Will replied, then waited for more, but Smith didn't offer. "You didn't do it?"

Smith sat up straight. "Let's just say the truth ain't always what it seems." He sighed. "Look, Buchanan, don't expect your innocence to save you. You get out of here, you've got no choice but to go after the bastard who did this to you."

The next morning Malvina arrived and informed him that a fat envelope containing twenty-five thousand cash in crisp hundred-dollar bills had arrived at the Saxton Mills Police Station the night before, along with an anonymous note explaining that it was for Will Buchanan's bail.

Chapter 11

THE QUESTION OF WHERE THE MONEY HAD COME FROM
dominated most of the conversation with Laurie at the police station Will's first night of freedom.

"I doubt whether the person who sent in the money did it
out of charity," Will said. "I mean, whoever it was must have
thought I was more valuable out than in."

"Somebody who has something to gain from your being
free?"

"Right. Suppose this person thinks I know where Erin is.
Wouldn't that be a good reason to bail me out?"

"And this person is, let's say, the one you saw skulking
about in the woods?"

"Well, yeah. Sure." He sat on the edge of her desk. "Any
leads on Erin?" he said.

"They found the car she stole in Concord."

"Well, that helps, doesn't it?"

"It was at the bus station."

"Oh."

"Exactly. North or south, your pick."

"No one remembers her buying a ticket?"

"No positive ID. Apparently a lot of teenage-girl traffic
that day."

"My guess is north," Will said. "She's around here somewhere."

"I hope you're right." She sipped her coffee. "God, I'm so
worried about her."

"I know."

"Whatever's going on, she's in way over her head."

Will stood. He placed a hand on Laurie's shoulder. "Let's just worry about what we know, okay?"

"I can't help it, though." She moved away from him.

"Ready to take a break?"

"I don't think I want to go out, Will."

"Come on. You said you'd help me celebrate my freedom."

"I know. I'm sorry. But it's probably not a good idea."

"You mean I have to drink on my own?"

"You shouldn't be drinking, Will. I'm certainly not going to sit in a restaurant and watch you violate your bail conditions."

"I was thinking more of having a nightcap at the house."

"I don't think you understand, Will. The rules are no drinking. Period."

"Even in the comfort of my own home?"

"Yes. You'd better not take this lightly. You could end up back in jail."

"You going to turn me in?"

"Probably not, but if someone else sees you drinking . . ."

"Okay. I get the point."

"Besides, I really have to clear up some of this work."

Will watched her as she pushed some paper around. She didn't look as busy as she claimed to be. "Well, as long as you're going to be slaving away, I might as well add to the workload," he said.

"That's okay. I've got more than I can handle."

"I think you should have a talk with Jackson Lloyd IV."

"About what?"

Will explained his seeing the newspaper photo with Jackson wearing a Rolex.

"You want me to call him down to the police station and question him about his watch?"

"Sure."

"I'd need a better reason than that."

"You could pull him in for speeding."

"Brilliant."

Will paused. "Let's just think this through a minute. Both Josh and his brother have similar Rolexes. Somebody's got to know about these watches."

"I'm not hauling him down here."

"Okay, I get it." Will thought a moment. "How about this? Call Kathryn and ask her if she knows anything about the watches. What's the harm in that?"

Laurie stared at him, then shook her head. "My God, Will. What's happened to you? You're starting to make sense."

"Prison has a way of focusing the mind."

––––––

The idea about contacting Kathryn had come upon Will suddenly, but it seemed logical as soon as he said it. Having seen the Rolex on Jackson's wrist made the watch he'd found at Zealand Falls appear in a completely new light, and all day long, since his morning release from the county jail, he could think of little else. He had been so fixated on the watch's belonging to Josh and on how Zippy had probably lied about his having worn it that he hadn't kept his mind open to other possibilities. With similar expensive watches involved now, shown clearly on the wrists of Kathryn's two sons, it would be unlikely that she wouldn't know anything about them.

Laurie placed the phone call immediately after Will's suggestion. She was lucky to catch Kathryn at home, for she was just headed out the door to visit a friend when the phone rang.

"It's a tradition in the Lloyd family," Kathryn said. "A gift from father to son when the son turns eighteen."

"Do you know if Josh was wearing his on the hiking trip?"

"No, I don't."

"Would you be willing to take a look at the one we found?"

"Sure. I'll drive up tomorrow and have a look."

Will made it a point to be at the station early, before Kathryn was scheduled to arrive. When Laurie placed the watch on the table in front of Kathryn, she immediately drew back.

"What is it?" Laurie said.

As she picked up the watch and examined it, tears began to form in her eyes.

"Is it Josh's?" Will asked.

"No," she said. "It's my husband's. It's Jacko's."

"Are you sure?" Laurie asked.

Will grabbed a box of tissues, pulled out a few, and handed them to Kathryn. His mind raced. The watch belonged to her former husband? His immediate thought was something he found difficult to believe.

Kathryn spoke his mind for him. "My God. You don't think Jacko's still alive?"

Laurie said, "How can you be positive this is really Jacko's watch?"

"Look," Kathryn said, pointing to a mark on the casing. "He scratched that by accident when we were on vacation once. He was so upset about it."

Will was taken aback, not only by the news but by the emotion Kathryn displayed. It was clear that, despite the divorce, she still loved her former husband.

"We found some numbers and letters inside the casing," Laurie said.

"Of course. That will prove it's his."

Laurie took out the slip of paper with the code written on it in block letters: 10JL2102JL358.

Kathryn used a pen as a pointer. "JL2 stands for Jackson Lloyd II."

"And JL3, Jackson Lloyd III," Laurie said.

"Right. JL2 2, meaning 'to,' JL3. Now read the numbers that are left," Kathryn said.

"Ten, ten, five, eight. Ten, ten, fifty-eight? Jackson Lloyd III's eighteenth birthday?"

She nodded. "Jacko's father was a nice man." She touched Laurie's arm. "You never met him, did you?"

Laurie shook her head no. "And Jacko continued the tradition with his sons?"

"Yes, as I told you on the phone. Each got a watch on his eighteenth birthday."

Will said, "Do they have similar codes on the casing?"

Kathryn nodded agreement. "Jacko's father was a careful, thorough man. He wanted a quick, easy identifier. Jacko was very much like him and used the same idea for the watches he gave to his sons."

Laurie asked, "Do you know if Jacko wore his watch all the time?"

"Always," Kathryn said. "He was careful with it. That's why he was so upset about the scratch on the casing."

It seemed so simple now that the story of the watches had

come out, but instead of feeling that he finally had some answers, Will was left with more questions. If this was indeed
Josh's father's watch, then what was it doing at Zealand Falls?
Could Jacko have faked his own death? And if it meant that
Josh's father was still alive, was he the one Will had seen in the
woods watching Josh and Erin go at it? And was it Jacko
who'd pushed his own son over the edge?

The main purpose of the Sunday-afternoon trip to the Lloyd
estate was simply to visit with Candace about Erin, at least to
offer some consolation, even if Laurie had little to give re-
garding her daughter's whereabouts. It was a trip she'd kept
putting off.

"Did you call ahead?" Will asked.

"No. I'm sure it's all right, though."

"We're just going to show up?"

"She's a recluse, Will. She's not going anywhere."

Will noticed as they drove that the foliage had gone past its
peak. Since his incarceration, leaves had fallen in multitudes,
and the early November light infused the sallow yellow and
dull browns with a soft radiance.

"I find it better not to let her know I'm coming," Laurie said.

"Why's that?"

"Because she worries about everything now. She would
spend the whole time waiting for us, thinking I'd gotten into
an accident."

"It's that bad?"

"Worse." Laurie turned off Interstate 93 at the Holderness
exit. "Thanks for coming along. Once again."

"That's okay. I admit, though, I'm concerned about meeting your sister."

"Don't be."

"I'm the man who's supposed to have raped her daughter. Remember?"

"That's why I want you to come along. I'm sure your being there will help show her it's not true."

"I don't know how."

"The bail money might help convince her of your innocence. Someone out there thinks you didn't do it and is willing to back it with cash." Laurie looked lost in thought. The front tire caught the edge of the highway, and she jerked the wheel to put the car back on course. "I just keep thinking about all that money," she said. "Who has twenty-five grand?"

"Especially to spend on me."

"Especially . . ."

"You don't have to agree with me."

"I didn't mean it that way. It's just that neither one of us knows anyone with that kind of money."

Will paused. "And you still don't think I raped Erin either. Right?"

"You know I don't."

"Sometimes I just need to hear it, I guess." Will paused. "I'm sure Malvina told you there might be reason to suspect she wasn't raped at all."

"Yes." She glanced over at him. "It doesn't change anything, though, at least for the time being. You're still accused of a felony, Will. Right now we have no other leads."

"Thanks for reminding me." In truth, Will was just pleased to have been invited along. Since his release he hadn't been sure how Laurie was going to react to his being back in her life. He sensed she was struggling to treat him as if nothing had happened, but that there was something there that prevented her from accepting it. He knew he had to find out what had really been going on with Erin if he ever hoped to regain any normalcy in their relationship.

"Did you see Kathryn's reaction when she picked up the watch and found it was Jacko's?"

"Yes. It was obviously a painful reminder."

"But what was so attractive about Jacko? I mean, here he had two women fighting over him. His loss obviously devastated both. Just look at how your sister reacted."

"It wasn't only his looks. Jacko had a quality about him that suggested he was a take-charge kind of guy, yet very loving at the same time. I think there were other women in his life before Candace."

"A ladies' man."

"Interesting expression."

"Tell me more about Candace," he said. "I know the bare bones about her life, but what is she like?"

"She won't bite, if that's what you mean."

"Well, is she depressed all the time? Does she, let's say, do things like laugh?"

"She tries to stay upbeat, but you can imagine how hard it is."

"Are you going to tell her about Jackson's watch?"

"I don't think so. Not now anyway."

"It's probably a good idea to keep it under wraps for a while."

"It's not like we're hiding anything. After all, we're not sure exactly what it means."

"It means either Jacko's alive and he was at Zealand Falls when Josh died or someone else had stolen Jacko's watch and lost it at Zealand Falls."

"Which one are you leaning toward?"

Will considered. "What I can't get out of my head are two things: one, the condition of the watch. It hadn't been out there long, no signs of being in the elements, and two, the broken band. It looked like it had been ripped off someone's wrist. The force must have been really something to break it at a link."

"There's one other thing."

"What's that?"

"I can't find any evidence that Jacko had, before his death, reported his watch stolen. I mean, if it meant as much to him as Kathryn claims, I'm sure he would have reported the theft."

"Do you think Kathryn is really going to be quiet about Jacko's watch?"

"I hope so. At least until we can find out more. I just don't want to give Candace any false hopes until we know for sure whether Jacko's alive. I'm sure it would kill her if it turned out we were wrong."

"I guess she really loved him. Probably as much as Kathryn. He must have been a hell of a guy."

"He was."

"What do you know about Erin's father?"

"The first husband? Just what I told you. That he turned into a violent control freak."

"Well, what about before?"

"I met him only once. I made a trip out west after Erin was born."

"Out west?"

"Utah. Candace met Harold, as I told you before, in college."

"She went to college in Utah?"

"No. Both went to Boston University. Harold had just come off a stint in the service. He was a Navy SEAL. "

"Ah. The elite."

"Candace fell for him right away, probably because he had Jacko's same take-charge qualities. She lacked self-confidence and found comfort in being taken care of."

"Unlike her sister."

Laurie smiled. "Well, I kind of like it when *you* take care of me."

"You do?"

"Of course."

"Then come back to the house and let me take care of you."

"There are others I have to take care of first."

"Let me help you."

She reached over and touched his leg. "You *are* helping me. Just by being here, you're helping."

He put his hand on top of hers.

"Anyway," she said, "let me finish my story." She pulled her hand away and placed it back on the wheel. "So Harold convinced Candace to drop out of school and go back to his hometown to live. She never did finish college."

"And she didn't like the wide-open spaces?"

Laurie pulled the cruiser onto a dirt road that Will remembered from when they'd attended Josh's memorial service. It led directly to the estate. "Everything seemed okay when I was out there," she said, "but Candace did confide in me that he seemed to change after they got out to Utah. Like I told you, he was apparently rediscovering his religion or something and wanted Candace to do the same."

"And Candace didn't?"

"No, she'd never been especially religious, and this seemed extreme to her. It was some kind of fundamentalism or something."

"So Harold must have really flipped when she left him."

"It happened quickly. As I told you, Jacko had prearranged her escape. It took a lot of guts to leave him. She had nightmares about him for years after."

"And when Candace lost Jacko, that's when she really fell apart."

Laurie drove through the open gate of the Lloyd estate and parked in front of the main house. "Don't be surprised if Candace looks a little thin to you. She hasn't been eating well."

———

Candace had long since moved from the carriage house into the main building. Will and Laurie were met at the door by Robert, a manservant who had been with the family since the days when Jackson II, Jacko's father, was head of the house. Jackson II was a stern Methodist, an eccentric inventor, who had built the estate on land he, in turn, had inherited from his father. The original Jackson, a logging magnate, made his fortune by stripping the White Mountains of timber, leaving behind slash and mud.

Robert was stooped from his years of service, and he walked with careful steps. He led them through the long hallway. The building was constructed from hand-hewn logs, the rafters rising like a vaulted wooden heaven above their heads. Will was sure the place must have been pleasant at one time, when it had been teeming with people—he tried to imagine Josh as a young boy running through the halls—but now it appeared as a void, the shadows thrown from the light of the fireplace in the great room especially accentuating the gloom. The place smelled dank, like day-old soup.

They followed Robert up the main stairwell, a trip that took some time given Robert's arthritic, crablike walk. Light from a half-open door spilled out into the hallway. Robert stood stiffly and announced their presence.

"Laurie, is it you?" The voice sounded reedy and thin.

Laurie gestured for Will to stay put. From the hallway he could barely hear the two sisters exchanging pleasantries. Robert waited outside the door with Will. Every now and again, Will caught Robert eyeing him.

Soon Laurie opened the door and nodded for Will to enter. Will approached the bed where Candace lay propped up against two of the largest pillows he'd ever seen. Laurie introduced him, and Candace held out her hand. Will took it but almost let it drop as soon as he felt the bones through the skin.

"No," she said. "You didn't rape my daughter."

"What?" Will said.

"Your eyes are kind, your hands gentle."

"That may be," Will said. "But it's true anyway. I didn't rape your daughter."

"I'm sorry for what Erin's put you through."

Will hadn't known what to expect, but her being so readily understanding came as a surprise.

"I'm sorry it's taken so long for me to come up and see you," Laurie said.

"I understand you're busy. I follow the news."

"Then you know that Erin has run away."

Candace placed her hands together. Will could see the white knuckles through the pale blue skin. "I told you that she would be trouble for you. I shouldn't have let you take her away from me."

Laurie said, "I didn't come here to argue. I just want you to know that I'm doing all I can to find her."

"I realize that. And I know it's not your fault."

Laurie touched her hand. "Are you getting enough to eat?"

"Yes. I think so. Everything tastes bland, though." She smiled. It looked as though it took some effort. "If food were a number, it would be zero."

"You have to eat, Candace."

"Robert takes good care of me."

Will watched her as she talked. Her dark hair, strands of gray interspersed, fell to her shoulders, framing an angular face with high cheekbones. She was too young to have that much gray hair.

As he stared at her, he thought of Laurie, of the courage it must have taken to move Erin away from this place and try to give her a normal life. It was clear there had been a fight over Laurie's taking her away, that it had been going on for a while, yet he'd known nothing about it. Will wondered if he and Laurie would ever get to a place where they could share their feelings with ease. He tried to suppress the sense that enveloped him now, that they would never make it together, two like-mannered, closed-off people, doomed to live separate lives even when they were together.

Laurie said, "Candace, do you have any idea where Erin might be?"

"No." Her voice grew soft. "She really has no place to run to."

Will felt like asking a few questions of his own, but he decided it was best not to butt in.

"She never mentioned a friend's house or any place like that?"

"No. That's why you took her away," Candace said. "She didn't have any friends, remember?"

"Okay, but if you think of anything, I'd appreciate it if you'd let me know." She touched Candace's hand. "Now I think we'd better be going. I'm upsetting you."

"You don't have to leave."

"I know seeing people tires you out."

"I'm sorry I'm so much trouble."

"Come on, Candace. Don't be this way, please?"

"I don't want you to leave. I get so lonely."

"I know. I'm sorry. But you need to start thinking about getting out of this house."

"I'm trying."

"How are your sessions going?"

"The doctor says I'm making progress." She picked some tissue from a dispenser on the nightstand. "I don't believe him, though. Robert still has to walk with me to the bathroom."

———

Robert had remained in the hallway and was waiting for them when they came out of the room.

Laurie whispered to him, "Is she really eating anything?"

"Not much," Robert said.

"She looks worse than when I last saw her."

"Her doctor is not helping her," Robert said.

Will was surprised by Robert's directness and immediately had a new respect for him. Robert had no doubt witnessed quite a bit in this household, and he apparently didn't suffer fools easily.

"I'll see if I can find some other doctor who knows something," Laurie said.

"Listen, Robert," Will said, "do you think you could show us Josh's room?"

Robert drew himself up straight. "I could, if you had a good reason for seeing it."

"When did he last live here?" Laurie asked.

Robert thought a moment. "Up until six months ago, when he started his hiking trip. He didn't spend much time in his room, though."

"You mean he didn't live at home?"

"He stayed with Erin in the carriage house."

They were halfway down the long staircase when Will turned to Laurie. "I think the picture of him and Erin was taken in front of the house. I recognize the siding in the background."

Laurie nodded agreement.

Will looked back at Robert. "Josh had a Rolex, didn't he?"

"He did."

"Do you know if he took it with him on the trip?"

Robert hesitated. "I don't know."

"I just wanted to take a look at his room to see if it's there," Will said.

"Well, if he didn't take it with him," Robert said, "I can tell you he wouldn't have left it in his room."

Will waited for more, but Robert seemed preoccupied with his thoughts.

"Where *would* he have put his watch, Robert?" Laurie said.

"In the safe, of course."

"Can you show us?"

"I need to get Ms. Candace's permission."

"Never mind," Laurie said. "I'll ask her." Laurie walked back up the stairs.

Will and Robert waited on the staircase for her return. Will said, "Did Candace know about Erin and Josh being lovers?"

"Yes, sir. It wasn't good."

"Did Laurie know? Is that why she got Erin out of here?"

"I don't think so. Ms. Candace didn't tell her, and she told me not to say anything, because she thought it was sinful."

"So Laurie *didn't* know they were lovers."

"She just thought this house wasn't a good place for Erin to be. She was right."

"Thank you, Robert."

"Yes, sir."

Laurie returned within a few minutes. "It's okay, Robert. I'm just not supposed to steal the family jewels."

When they reached the large mahogany-paneled living room at the center of the house, Robert instructed, "You two stay here. I'll check the safe." He turned and headed toward a part of the house Will had not seen.

"Let's hope the safe isn't hidden in the cellar somewhere," Will said. "Robert might never return."

"It's a wonder he's still here," Laurie said. "I don't know what I'd do without him."

"I love you," Will said.

"What? What brought that on?"

"It's just that now I know better what you've been going through," he said. "You didn't need to move out of the house because of this. I think I could have adjusted to having Erin around."

"Okay. But it's too late to fix that."

"So does that mean you're going to move back in?"

Before Laurie could answer, Robert returned. "Is this what you're looking for?" he asked. He held a Rolex in his hand and showed it to Will. It looked like the one in the photo, but, if Kathryn was right, there should be a code in the casing to confirm it.

"Can we borrow this for a while, Robert?" Laurie said. "It might help us figure out what happened to Josh."

"Just tell Miss Candace you're taking it," he said.

On the way out the door, Will turned to Laurie and said, "Looks like Zippy was telling the truth."

Laurie frowned, as if remembering her misgivings about Josh's trail mate. "I'm still not ready to dismiss him," she said. "He's just too close to the action."

Chapter 12

IN THE CAR ON THE WAY BACK HOME, LAURIE SAID TO Will, "So what happens with you now?"

"You mean, am I going back to work?"

"Yes."

"I don't know if they'll let me. I have a meeting with Perry tomorrow."

"I think it would be good for you to get right back in harness, and I hope Perry sees it that way."

He shifted in his seat so he could look at Laurie directly. "You know what I think *you* should do next?"

"I'm sure you're going to tell me."

"Take a look at Erin's computer."

"What for?"

Will told her about Kendra's description of how Erin worked into the night and disturbed her sleep. "I just think she might have written something about what she was going through."

"I'll get on it tomorrow."

"Why don't you let me take care of it?"

Laurie shook her head. "It's not your job."

"Come on. There's too much work for you to do alone. Let me talk to the school's computer guy."

"Merrill Fogarty? That gossip!"

"If there's anything on Erin's hard drive, he can find it."

"I think you've done enough, Will. And I can't take any more guilt from having gotten you into this mess in the first place."

"You're saying you don't want my help?"

Laurie looked to be considering her words carefully. "Things have changed, Will. You may be out of jail, but you're not out of the woods."

"What's that supposed to mean?"

"Means that the judge would not appreciate your playing detective. You're on a tight leash, remember?"

Will turned away from her and stared out the window. They had just passed the Squam Lakes Science Center. "You don't expect me to sit around on my hands."

"That's exactly what I expect you to do. For your own sake."

"You need my help, Laurie."

Laurie took a corner hard and punched the accelerator. "I need your support. There's a difference."

"No, you need me to trade off ideas. I'm a good sounding board. If it hadn't been for me, we wouldn't have found out about the Rolexes."

"Okay. I'll give you that."

"Do you really still think Zippy might be involved in this?" As they drove through Ashland, in the light cast from the storefronts, Will could see her mouth still set tight from their visit.

"I don't know," she said. "Maybe I just don't like him."

"You see? That's not a good answer. You need me to keep you honest."

"Apparently you're not hearing me."

"I hear you fine."

"You could end up back in jail."

"All I'm doing is offering my help."

"You're a science teacher, not a policeman."

"I love you . . . and I want to help Erin."

Will waited for a response, but none came. He was hoping

his last remark would soften her resolve, but it seemed to have little effect. He put his arm over the back of the seat and tried to sound casual. "Okay, I understand where you're coming from, but you're not hearing me either."

Laurie looked away from him.

"Come on," Will said.

"You are not going to be involved in this investigation any further," she said, her eyes trained on the windshield.

Will suddenly recalled Smith's cell-block advice about not relying on his innocence alone. "All right. I may not be a cop, but I'm also not going to roll over and play dead when my life and reputation are threatened. If there's something I can do to clear my name, I'm going to do it."

"Nice speech," she said. "I just hope you don't do something you'll regret."

———

The next morning, after a welcome night of sleeping in his own bed, Will woke up thinking about Smith still in jail. Was Smith telling the truth about being falsely accused of killing his best friend? Prisons were supposedly full of guilty people convinced of their own innocence. But there was something in Smith's voice that suggested he was telling the truth. Maybe when this was all over, Will would go back and visit him to get the full story.

The morning sunlight lifted Will's spirits, and he was convinced he could carry on with his life right where he'd left off, but as he drove onto campus for his appointment with Perry, conscious of people staring at his car, he was no longer sure he could return to his teaching. The thought of pretending that everything was fine all day long in the classroom seemed too tiring even to consider.

It didn't take too much convincing for Perry to agree with him, and his ready compliance took Will by surprise. "I thought you'd at least give me the option to come back if I wanted to," he said.

Perry sat down in his desk chair. He pushed a strand of hair back off his forehead. "That would be nice. But I'm sure you realize it's a bit more complicated."

"What's complicated?" Will said. "I'm accused of a crime. I haven't been convicted yet. Seems to me I should have the option to return to work if I want to."

"I thought you didn't want to 'fake it.' I think that's the way you put it."

"I don't. I just want to have the option to fake it."

"This whole thing is a mess," Perry said. He made a tent with his fingers. "Made even messier since it involves one of our students."

"You mean if I'd raped an old lady, I could still teach if I wanted to?"

"Don't be ridiculous, Will."

Will didn't like the way this conversation was heading. He sat forward, anxious suddenly that Perry was working on a preset agenda. "So you're firing my ass. Is that what this is about?"

Perry got up from his chair. He walked to a window and stood for a moment, his hands clasped behind his back. "A leave of absence." He turned and faced Will. "I'm sorry, but there's little else I can do."

"With pay?"

"Of course, with pay."

"Is this your decision or the board's?"

"Both."

"I thought the board was going to come up with my bail money. What happened to all their understanding and sensitivity?"

"There's a difference, Will. I'm sure you see it. We have to think of the entire school community, parents included, and not just you."

Will let Perry's words sink in. "Okay, I think I got it. The money is quiet, just the rustle of paper, but allowing the country rapist back into the henhouse—well, that shouts of something else: actual belief in my innocence."

"I don't think I would have put it that way."

"Put it any way you want, Perry. Better yet, stick it anywhere you want."

Perry's face colored, and Will could tell by the way his hands were squeezed together that he was struggling to maintain his composure. His knuckles were turning red.

Time to defuse. Will sat back in his chair. "Look, Perry, I'm sorry. I didn't mean that."

"I think you did."

"Well, then at least I shouldn't have said it."

"What makes this so hard," Perry said, "is that we're friends first."

"I know. And I understand this hasn't been easy on you." Will looked up and met his eyes. "But it hasn't exactly been a picnic for me."

"I'm sure the truth will come out."

"But I am accused of something, and I really have no defense."

"Give it time, Will."

"Don't tell me that," Will said. "You know, my lawyer was right. It doesn't matter if I'm innocent or not. I'm treated as if I'm guilty."

"I'm sorry it has to be that way." Perry paused. He opened his jacket and let his hands rest on his hips. "Seems like we've been here before."

It took a moment for Will to catch on. "You mean with Dee Tyler?"

"Yes."

"Yeah, it sounds familiar. I guess every few years I need to make your life interesting."

Perry attempted a smile. "Don't knock yourself out."

"I just wish I knew where Erin was."

"We all do."

"One thing for sure: None of this is going away until we find her."

Perry rubbed the back of his neck. "Anything I can do to help, let me know."

Will almost dismissed the suggestion, but then he realized that he might be able to use Perry's authority. "You serious about that?"

"Of course."

"I need to borrow Merrill Fogarty for a while." Will described Kendra's description of Erin madly typing in the middle of the night.

"You just want to check out her computer?"

"That's it."

Perry looked as if he were running through all the possibilities for lawsuits. Finally he said, "I don't see any harm."

"I'd like to look at it now, if I could."

Perry picked up the phone. "I'll see if Merrill's in."

"Could you tell him to meet me in Erin's dorm?"

"Sure."

The arrangements were made quickly. Merrill, one of the busiest men on campus, just happened to be in between computer crises. Will got up from his chair and strode across the room. He shook Perry's hand. "Thanks for your help."

"Let me know what you find."

Will headed toward the door, then stopped, his hand on the knob. He faced Perry. "I need to know something before I leave. Do you think I raped Erin?"

"No."

"Honest?"

"Honest."

———

Will wanted Perry to initiate the meeting with Merrill, not only because it meant that the arrangement would come from on high but also because he wouldn't have to walk all over campus, being gawked at by students and colleagues, as he tried to track Merrill down. Will didn't exactly skulk to Erin's dorm, but he took a back way around the heating plant, a less populated route.

The sky was gray and dull and matched his monochrome mood. Will wasn't really angry over being forced into a leave of absence, which surprised him. The truth was, he felt relieved, knowing he really couldn't have pretended things were normal in the class for very long, and his conversation with Perry helped clarify exactly what he had to do: He had to find Erin, and he had to do it despite Laurie's or anyone else's objections. He knew it would mean risking all the progress he'd made with Laurie, but right now that didn't seem to matter as much as saving his hide. He resented the idea that there had to be a trade-off, though.

What he also couldn't reconcile was that the more this nightmare was left to run its course, the more guilty he actually began to feel. It was as if he had to keep reminding himself that he really *didn't* rape Erin, had to keep asking people what they thought just to corroborate it. He remembered Malvina's response to his protestations of being innocent. "We all are," she'd said. Well, maybe she got it wrong. Maybe we're all guilty.

Will was able to make it into Erin's dorm through the rear door. It was after nine, and students were in class. He waited outside Erin's room for Merrill to show. As the computer guy, Merrill had access to everything on campus. He would have a key.

Will looked out the window in the hallway, hoping that one of the girls in the dorm wasn't bedridden and would come upon him on her way to the bathroom. He didn't want to explain anything. He was beyond explanations. Blessedly, Merrill soon drove up in his truck.

Will had always liked Merrill, mainly because he could talk with him—if he could find a way to jump into the rare pauses—about books and real life. Merrill's background was in music, not science. Laurie's assessment of him as a gossip was accurate. Need to spread a rumor? Go to Merrill. Will was sure that Merrill would probably blab about his wanting to look at Erin's computer, but it seemed a small price to pay if the hard drive yielded information about where she might be. Besides, he had permission from Perry to look at it.

Will recalled one interesting discussion about the relation-

ship of music and computers. "Computers are mathematical,"
Merrill had said. "But so is music. The problem is that you
can't approach music like a math problem without its sounding stiff and mechanical. You need to feel it, just like you
need to feel computers. Understanding how they work is
really intuitive and spatial. You've got to think horizontally,
not vertically."

Coming down the hallway, Merrill himself appeared more
horizontal than vertical. He was a squat man. Merrill fumbled
with keys as he walked toward Will, humming a tune Will
recognized as the *Masterpiece Theatre* theme.

"Well, Buchanan," he said as he approached, "I guess you've
been up to your ass in alligators." He shook Will's hand.

"Been keeping up with me, Merrill?"

He winked. "Someday you'll have to tell me all about the
county jail."

"Everything?"

"Details, Buchanan. Details."

"Thanks for doing this, Merrill."

"Hey, if it helps . . ." He found the right master and un-
locked the door. "You know what you're looking for?"

"Not really."

He winked again, an irritating habit. "Just want to do
some snooping, eh? Well, I'll tell you, you never know what
you're going to find with these kids—but I don't have to tell
you that, right? You know what I'm talking about. You teach
them. Hell, you should have seen the porn some kid down-
loaded last night! Boy, is he in trouble!"

Merrill's penchant for running his mouth meant that Will
would do a lot of nodding, but that was okay. Just as long as
he could interrupt him long enough to tap his expertise.

Erin's side of the room looked as if it hadn't been touched. The picture of her and Josh stood on her dresser. Laurie must have returned it immediately after having it copied, and it seemed now as eerie as an old daguerreotype of relatives who have long since passed.

Merrill sat down and fired up Erin's computer, an older-model Macintosh Power PC, as Will described what Kendra had said about Erin's working late at night. Will pulled up Kendra's desk chair beside Merrill, who quickly double-clicked and opened her hard drive. "My God," he said.

Will saw immediately what Merrill was reacting to. It was the complete lack of volume on the hard drive. There were a total of nine word-processing files, and they all looked like schoolwork.

"See anything appealing?" Merrill said.

Will went down the list of file names: "Red Badge Essay," "Hist. Notes," "Dumb Chem."

"At least she uses Microsoft Office," Merrill said. "Like using a howitzer to kill a flea, though." He turned and looked at Will. "Want to see what's here?"

Will nodded. "Won't take us long anyway."

As Merrill clicked through the files, Will began to sink lower in his chair. Nothing. The files were all less than two pages long.

"She must have deleted everything," Merrill said.

"Is there any way to get it back?"

"I could try some stuff. I'll need to take the computer with me, though."

"Is that legal?"

"The school owns the network, and it's my job to police it. If you want me to, I'll check it out with Perry first."

"No. He's already authorized the search. See what you can find."

Will's disappointment over the lack of information on the hard drive rested like a heavy weight on his shoulders. He had expected the computer to be a window into Erin's troubled mind, not a blank screen.

———

At first, Will thought he might go home, but the thought of being in the house alone smacked of waiting around for things to happen to him. What else could he do? He had counted on having Erin's computer occupy most of his time as he searched her files for hints that would reveal her whereabouts. Why did she delete everything? Was she that worried that people would read what Will imagined as her most intimate thoughts?

As he drove through town, he couldn't get Erin out of his mind. He kept coming back to the idea that if Erin was still alive, she had to be in a place she knew well. She'd grown up on the Lloyd estate, after all, and was familiar with that part of New Hampshire. His gut sense told him she was close by—*if* she was still alive. At the outskirts of town, he doubled back and parked his truck in front of the town library.

He was still driving his '79 Dodge Ram 4x4, and right now he wished he had a vehicle that was less recognizable. He'd torn off the old bed when it had rotted out and built a new one of pressure-treated lumber. People would know he was in town.

The library was in a retrofitted Odd Fellows Hall. The copper door handle was shiny from use, and Will pulled open the heavy door. He strode to the main desk and found Alice Defoe at a computer. "Morning, Alice."

She looked up at him over half glasses. Her blue hair looked as if it had been freshly permed. "Hello, Will." There was a sharp look of recognition first, then a relaxing of her shoulders. Will guessed she was feigning ease with his being there. "How can I help you?" she asked.

"Do you have newspapers that go back a few years?"

"We have them on fiche."

"I want to read up on Jackson Lloyd."

Alice paused, looking as if she were doing mental arithmetic: Will Buchanan plus Jackson Lloyd equals trouble. "Follow me," she said.

In one of the side rooms, Will sat down in front of a microfiche reader while Alice searched the database on a nearby computer. He was counting on there being more than just a skinny obit on Jackson, especially given the fact that his body had never been found.

Will knew it wouldn't take Alice long. He had learned long ago that good librarians live fervently for helping people find things, and the best way to get results was to let them do their job. He had used Alice's skills before, and now it took less than ten minutes before he was reading an article in the same Conway weekly where he'd seen the picture of Jacko's son, Jackson Lloyd, and his Rolex.

The article attempted to piece together Jacko's last day, as if emphasizing that each step would be the key to yielding some clue as to how his canoe came to be upside down in a lake on his property. Will recognized the name on the byline: George Archer. Will liked his work.

While the description of Jacko's last day was thorough, it became clear as Will read the article that there was little more than speculation as to what had happened. Jacko was supposed to have gone to his hunting camp in the morning to make some repairs on a window that had been busted. This is what he'd told his family. Sometime during the day, he put his canoe into the rushing stream that emptied out at a pond about two miles below the camp. There was no answer given as to why he would do that if the main reason for going to the camp was to fix a window.

Jacko liked to fish, but no tackle was found when divers searched the pond. No body. Just an upturned canoe.

Archer had gone to the trouble of drawing a map of the area, showing the relationship of the hunting camp to the pond, with the stream connecting the two. The map was not drawn to scale, but Will knew enough of the area to approximate where that camp might be.

It looked like a perfect place to hide out.

Chapter 13

WILL'S MOOD IMPROVED AS HE HEADED OUT TO THE
Lloyd estate. He trusted that Erin would have known about
this hunting camp. Josh must have been familiar with it, his
father certainly introducing him to hunting early in life. And
it sounded like a good trysting place, somewhere Josh could
have taken Erin to be away from the house.

Will found a dirt road that dead-ended at an earth berm
about a mile in near the south end of the pond. He took it as
a good sign that he was able to park the truck off the main
drag—less likely to be noticed. He got out of the cab and
studied the sky. It was almost noon. He figured it would take
about two hours to get to the camp, and he would have
plenty of light left for his return.

A path led in from the dead end. The wind gusted, whoosh-
ing through the tops of the fir stand. The sky looked as if it
was beginning to clear, the clouds skirting in and out of sun-
shine.

It felt good to stretch his legs. The path soon led to the
mouth of the stream where it emptied into the pond, surging
strongly now from recent rains. Archer's map was just a simple construction, and there had been no need to have it du-
plicated. Will had it in his head.

He stood on a boulder, took out his compass, and checked
his bearings. If he followed the stream in, it should lead directly to the camp. The path petered out at the mouth of the
pond. He would have to bushwhack in.

The going near the stream was fairly easy, and Will stuck close to it, rock-hopping as he went. He'd been walking for more than an hour when his stomach rumbled, reminding him he hadn't eaten since last night. He realized that he'd been so focused on his task that he hadn't thought about anything else.

But he made good time, pausing every now and again to look at his compass. It was clear the area hadn't been logged in a while, and he estimated there was enough timber to keep the Lloyd clan in dough for another century. Why they were even considering a ski area was beyond him. Besides pine, there was plenty of red oak and maple. Getting it out, though, would cut up the land, but he imagined that a ski area would do worse damage.

The stream flowed steadily, the swift current providing a direct and challenging ride for any canoeist. This was not a course for a Sunday outing.

A little more than an hour in, the water pooled and calmed. The sky had cleared to a bright blue, and the sun was warm on his face. Will figured that the hunting camp should be close by. He strained his eyes upstream. He was about to move on when, across the water, something flashed and interrupted his concentration.

Will studied the opposite shore, but he could see nothing out of order. It was one of those momentary happenings that he was not sure, upon reflection, had actually occurred—a glint off something shiny that his gut told him wasn't part of the natural setting. It stuck in the back of Will's mind as he made his way upstream. Finally he came upon the camp.

He approached carefully from the rear, choosing an

oblique route. If Erin was in the cabin, she might not be alone. He listened but heard nothing. He sidled, his back against the building, toward the front.

The door was locked, but a window was broken. On Jacko's last day, he probably never had a chance to fix it. Will looked through the broken glass. The interior was rustic, but not without amenities—a sizable woodstove, bunks with thick mattresses, and several oil lamps. But the place was empty, and it didn't look as if anyone had been there for a while. Cobwebs laced the room, and squirrels had taken up residence.

He brushed off an Adirondack chair on the front porch of the cabin, sat down, and looked out over the stream. He had struck out with Erin's computer, and now, when he'd been so sure he would find something, he had whiffed again.

Will struggled with what his next step should be. He still had the feeling that if he could just find one piece of information, a loose thread, then the rest of the truth would unravel.

He got up from his chair and started exploring around the cabin. Maybe he'd missed something. He discovered an outhouse but little else. It had been a long time since Jacko had disappeared, and Will didn't really expect to uncover anything that might shed light on what happened that day, but he had learned long ago that the truth often revealed itself in unexpected places. The important thing was to keep his eyes open.

He ventured across the stream to where there was a small dock and a canoe upside down on sawhorses, a cheap one made of aluminum, not like the top-of-the-line Old Town found capsized in the pond downstream.

It was swampy a few yards in from the stream, and Will dropped to one knee when he spotted an impression in the mud. At first he thought it might be the paw print of a bear—it was large enough—but closer inspection revealed a lug sole, about size twelve, he estimated. And the print was fresh.

Will stood suddenly. He scanned the woods but could see nothing unusual. He followed the prints for a while. They led down the opposite side of the stream.

And the glint? Yes, he had seen it. It might have been the reflection off a pair of sunglasses. There was no doubt someone had followed him in. It made him angry that he hadn't caught on to the fact earlier.

Will decided to track the footprints. With any luck he might catch up to whoever had trailed him. He picked up his pace, stumbling a few times where the underbrush grew heavy, cursing to himself over his clumsy foot placement.

The prints led all the way back down to the pond and veered off on the path that led to Will's truck. He began to scurry along the path, fearful that his truck might be gone. He had the terrible habit of leaving his keys in the ignition because he hated carrying things in his pockets.

But the truck was there, as well as the keys. Will checked the cab. The detritus on the seat had shifted. Someone had rifled through his stuff.

He slammed the door of the cab, and when that didn't help his fuming, opened it one more time and slammed it again.

————

The next morning Will turned his truck into the parking lot of The Mountaineer, a diner located at the south end of Saxton Mills. Just reopened, the place had changed hands many times. The new owners were pushing ample portions of good food in a completely nonsmoking atmosphere. The business tactic seemed to be working. Will had to settle for a space at the counter.

Coming in, he'd noticed a poster with Erin's picture on it hanging on the cash-register stand with HAVE YOU SEEN ERIN? in big block letters.

The coffee was hot and black, diner premium, and Will placed both hands around his cup while he waited for his eggs with hash browns and onions to arrive. His hands were still cold from scraping the frost off the windshield. It wouldn't be long until winter arrived.

In the background the radio played Sly & the Family Stone from the easy-listening Mount Washington station. Will gradually warmed to the crowded diner. If he closed his eyes, he could almost believe that he was just like these people, leading uneventful but enviable lives.

He was well into his second over-easy when the ten-o'clock news came on. More trouble in Afghanistan and another school shooting. Will took a bite of his sourdough toast. After a commercial for dandruff shampoo, it was time for the local news: "Surveyors working near the site of a proposed ski area on the Jackson Lloyd property earlier this morning discovered a badly decomposed body in a shallow grave at the foot of Hunger Mountain. Authorities would not speculate on the identity of the victim until forensic evidence can be examined."

Will rose from his stool. He took a gulp of his coffee, threw a ten-dollar bill on the counter, and headed out the door.

He drove past the police station first to make sure the cruiser was gone. He guessed that Laurie was on site at this moment and figured that the staging area of the investigation would be on the northern end, where there was a lumber road that led into the base of Hunger Mountain. He guessed right. When he turned off the main drag onto the lumber road, he was immediately met by a statie guarding the entrance in his cruiser. Will got out of his truck, bent down, and spoke through the passenger-side window. He told the cop he was looking for Laurie.

"She's up ahead talking with the ME."

"I need to see her."

The trooper studied him, and then there was a flash of recognition. "You're Buchanan, aren't you?"

"That's right."

"Sorry. I can't let you by." The trooper, full of spit and polish, acted like a by-the-book rookie.

"Can you just call her and tell her I'm here?" he said.

The trooper looked momentarily at the radio, then back to Will. "Why don't you just wait for her. I'm sure she won't be long."

Will sensed that there was little room to argue. The kid clearly wasn't interested in doing anything to bring his job of guarding the gate into question. "Thanks," he said.

Will backed up the truck and parked alongside the highway. He didn't know how far in the body was, and he really didn't feel like sitting in his truck for hours. He'd give it fifteen minutes. He couldn't quell the urge to be on the scene. He guessed there wasn't much hope of his actually seeing the body, but being there with those processing the information about the crime would be invaluable. He looked at his watch.

In another five minutes he would bushwhack around the officer at the gate and walk in.

He was about to get out of the cab when he heard tires on gravel. The Major Crime Unit van pulled out onto the highway and sped past him. The van was followed by ME Amy Liu in her state car. Laurie soon brought up the rear in her cruiser.

Will got out of the truck and waved Laurie over. She slowly passed him, and Will wasn't sure for a minute whether she was going to stop. A few yards up the road, she pulled over.

Will ran to the cruiser and got into the front seat. "I heard about it on the radio," Will said.

"Good for you," Laurie said. "But what are you doing here?"

"Is it Jacko's body?"

"I don't know. It might be."

"Pretty bad condition?"

"You could say that."

Laurie was her ramrod professional self, and Will knew it would take an effort to get anything out of her.

"What about his clothes?"

"There's plenty of forensic data, Will," she said. "Now, get out of the car."

"Look, I know you think I'm butting in—"

"I don't *think* anything. I *know* you are." She paused. "And what were you doing looking at Erin's computer with Merrill Fogarty?"

"I thought I'd find something."

"I told you that I'd take care of that."

"I'm just trying to help," he said.

She paused "Look, Will, I don't know exactly how to say this, but I guess you need to know where I'm coming from."

"I'm listening."

"I can't be with you now. Not the way things are. You're up to your ears in this, and I can't do my job and love you at the same time."

Will studied her face. "So when you order me out of the car, it's your way of saying you love me?"

"That's right. First, it's the best thing for you. And second, it's easier that way."

"Easier?"

"To be blunt. To keep you at arm's length. To keep me from getting confused. If you haven't caught on by now, I need things in little boxes. God, how else can I say it?"

"I don't know. You're not exactly easy to read."

"I can accept that. But neither are you."

"I guess we make a great couple."

Neither spoke for a few moments. Finally Laurie said, "I've never stopped loving you—that's the problem."

Her response was exactly what he wanted to hear, but it was so unexpected that he was at a loss for words.

"Now, out of the car."

"Say it like you love me."

"Get out of the car. Please."

———

The next day he cleaned the house for the first time since Laurie had left. The dust balls were the size of tumbleweeds. He hadn't felt up to the task before because he hadn't been sure there was a chance that Laurie would return, but now he attacked the house with gusto.

He had driven up to the Hunger Mountain site with the

hope of finding out about the body, but he'd come away with something much more important: the reassurance that Laurie still loved him—no, had never stopped loving him.

————

The housecleaning also helped take his mind off the upcoming hearing, just two short days away. He was worried and uncertain, despite Malvina's reassurances that there was little evidence against him. She was sure to get a stay until such time as Erin could be found. This was clearly a case of he said/she said.

Just before Will was about to turn in for the evening, he was surprised by the lights of a car pulling up. At first he thought it was Laurie driving up in the cruiser, and he was disappointed to see Ray Flemmer, her deputy.

Will met him on the front porch. "What's up, Ray? Here to arrest me again?"

"Has Laurie been here?"

"You mean today?"

"Yes."

"No. Why? What's wrong?"

"Well, I'm not sure anything is. I was just hoping I might find her here."

"Are you saying she's missing?"

"She hasn't come back yet. That's all I know."

Chapter 14

AT THE POLICE STATION, WILL TRIED TO GET RAY TO open up. "Are you sure you didn't know what she'd been working on?"

"She was following up on a lead; that's what her note said. I think somebody called in about seeing Erin's poster."

"But you don't know who?"

"She never told me."

"Don't you two work together on these things?"

"Sure. But I was handling traffic down where they're laying that new conduit when she got the call. Her note said she'd be back in the afternoon. When she didn't show, I started to worry. She always debriefs me around seven when my shift ends."

"God, Ray. Why didn't you call me earlier?"

"You're the last one I wanted to call." Ray stared at his shoes. "Laurie told me that if you came down to the police station for anything to do with Erin, I was to get rid of you fast. But I figured you should know about this."

"I'm glad you finally got hold of me."

"I still don't know if I should have. Man, she can be ornery sometimes."

"Listen, Ray," he said, "you'd better call the state police and report her missing. She was in her cruiser, right?"

"That's right."

"Well, that's something anyway. It would be hard to miss."

"And I should probably contact the phone company and check on the records for the day. That call must have come in this morning."

"Great." Will slapped him on the shoulder. "Good think-ing, Ray."

———

It took less than a half hour for Ray to place the calls. Will felt better knowing that the state police were on high alert for Laurie's cruiser. The check of the phone records revealed that four calls had come into the police station that morning: two from a police barracks out of state, one from a local school, and one from an RV campground. Of the four, Will's hunch was that the RV place was where Laurie had gone to follow up on the lead. "That must be it," Will said. "Let's go check it out."

"You're not going anywhere."

"Damn it, Ray. Laurie's missing. Let's get moving."

The RV campground was less than a half hour from Sax-ton Mills on the road to Conway. Will had passed it many times. It was a large park that boasted views of Mount Chocorua from every site. Ray pulled in. The place felt de-serted except for one light in the window of a small cottage set back from the road.

"Wait in the car," Ray said.

"I didn't come with you to wait in the car."

"Well, let me do the talking, then."

"You're the man, Ray."

Ray rapped on the cottage's screen door. It took several minutes for a response. Will guessed that the woman who came to the door was in her sixties. She had rollers in her hair and wore a floor-length bathrobe that looked fashioned from an old bedspread. She peered at them through glasses much too large for her face.

Ray pointed to his badge.

She opened the main door but kept the screen locked. "Is there something wrong?"

"I'm Officer Flemmer, ma'am. Did you make a call to the police station this morning?"

"I did."

"And did Officer Eberly come to talk with you?"

She nodded. "We had a nice chat."

"Do you mind if we come in, ma'am?" Ray said. "I know it's late, but I promise not to take up too much of your time."

The woman undid the latch and pulled on the screen door. It stuck near the top, and it took some doing for her to get it open. "That darned door," she said. "Since my husband died, the place has gone to hell." She led them into a small kitchen where there was a dinette table covered with a red-checkered oilcloth. "Would you fellas like a cup of tea?"

"No, ma'am," Ray said. "Are you Mrs. Miller?"

"Carmen," she said. "Call me Carmen."

Will and Ray shared one of the dinette benches. "So what time did Officer Eberly come to see you today?" Ray said.

"Just before lunch," Carmen said, putting on the kettle.

"And why did you call the police station in the first place?"

"I think I saw the girl that's missing."

"You saw her here?"

"That's right. I don't sleep well now that Elwood's passed. I'm pretty sure she got out of a car with a man and went into his trailer."

"And how long ago was that, ma'am?"

"About a week and a half."

"My name's Will, Carmen." Ray shot him a glance meant to shut him up, but Will continued. "Can you tell us something about the man she was with?"

"He's about six feet, kind of a muscular guy, you know."

"About her age, you'd say?"

She shook her head. "No, much older. Nice man."

"And you only saw this girl that looked like Erin once?" Ray asked.

"That's it. I remember being surprised to see her, you know. It was late, and Mr. Rothchild usually turned in pretty early."

"That's his name?" Will asked. "The one who was with Erin?"

"That's right."

"And he was usually by himself?"

"Yes."

"I wonder if I could trouble you for the registration form, ma'am," Ray said. "We'd be interested in how Mr. Rothchild filled in the blanks."

"I'd be pleased to give it to you, but Officer Eberly took it with her this morning."

Ray let out some air, clearly disappointed in the news.

"Is Officer Eberly all right?" Carmen asked. "Is that what this is about?"

"I'm afraid she's missing," Will said. Saying it aloud had the effect of making it sound unreal. He felt a sudden rise in anger. Someone had watched Laurie come in and followed her after she'd left the RV park. There was no doubt she'd been onto something. "Can we take a look at Mr. Rothchild's trailer, Carmen?" Will said.

"It's no longer here. He checked out a few days ago."

"Did he say where he was going?" Ray asked.

"No. He seemed in kind of a hurry, though."

"You mean he just took off?" Will asked.

"Well, he paid in cash and didn't wait around for the change. He was gone before I knew it."

"What sort of camper was it?" Ray asked.

"One of those fifth-wheelers. Small one, though."

"Do you remember anything about what was on that form?" Ray asked.

The teakettle sang, and Carmen pulled it off the stove. "You sure I can't give you gentlemen some tea?"

"None for me," Will said.

Carmen took her time putting loose tea in a tea ball. The brewing of the tea obviously involved important rituals. She brought her cup to the table, a saucer covering the top. "I can tell you his license plate was from Connecticut."

"I don't suppose you remember the number," Ray said.

Carmen thought a moment. "I can give you some of it," she said. "It began with twelve twenty-three. I remember because it's my birthday. There was also an R somewhere." She took the saucer off the top of the cup and removed the tea ball. "Oh, dear. I do hope Officer Eberly is okay."

"Yes, ma'am," Ray said. "We hope so, too."

"Did she say where she might be going next?" Will asked.

"You mean after she left me?"

"That's right."

"No. She was just grateful for what I could tell her." She blew across the top of the cup.

"And what you told her is pretty much what you've said to us?" Ray asked.

"Yes."

Will asked, "How long was this Mr. Rothchild hooked up here?"

She sipped her tea. "About six weeks."

The time frame fit. This could have been the man he'd seen disappearing into the woods at Zealand Falls. And most likely the one who had followed him to the hunting camp. The RV park would have made a good base of operations.

"I wonder if Mr. Rothchild meant to leave so much money," Carmen said. "Do you think I'd get into trouble if I spend it?"

"How much was it?" Will said.

"A hundred dollars over what I charged him," Carmen said. "I think that's a pretty good tip, don't you?"

———

By the time Will and Ray had finished interviewing Carmen, it was four in the morning. Will made it back to his house just as the sun was coming up. He found a call waiting for him on his answering machine. It was from Malvina Lincoln, reminding him that his probable-cause hearing was set for tomorrow and that it might be a good idea for them to huddle beforehand. She'd appreciate it if he called back. She ended with the hope that he was keeping his nose clean and promised that this whole thing would be over soon.

Will doubted it. It seemed like it was just beginning.

He struggled to the bedroom and tried to sleep, but his eyes flicked open every time he tried to close them. He kept imagining Laurie tied up somewhere or locked in a room. He felt she was so tantalizingly close by, but there was so little to go on that she might as well be on the moon. He just hoped she was still alive.

He soon drifted, only to be awakened by the phone around 7:00 A.M. It was Merrill Fogarty.

"I hope it's not too early."

"What's up, Merrill?"

"I think I found something."

Groggy from sleep, Will took a while to process what he was saying. "What are you talking about?"

"Erin's hard drive."

Will sat bolt upright. "Are you sure?"

"I was able to retrieve some of the stuff she deleted. I don't think I got all of it, but at least there's more than what you saw."

"I'll be right down."

The computer room at the Saxton Mills School was in the basement of one of the oldest buildings on campus, a converted barn that was part of the original estate that had once served as one of the state's largest milking parlors.

Will wondered, as he headed toward Merrill's lair, what it was about computers that always forced them into the bowels of buildings. He was grateful that the school day hadn't really begun and that he was able to slip downstairs without running into anyone.

Merrill was in the back room, hunched over Erin's computer. "What have you got, Merrill?" Will asked.

"Well, I'm not sure. It's gibberish." Merrill seemed more subdued than usual. "Some of it's actually kinda scary."

Will looked over his shoulder and began reading: *He's here now and I know what he wants me to do and I know that I'll never do it because it means I might as well be dead but he says he'll kill me but I don't believe him because he also says he loves me but mom he says he'll kill mom he'll*—and the file ended.

"Is that it?" Will said.

"No, there's more. Not much, though." Merrill punched up another file: *I can always go to Valhalla I will be safe there where he can't get to me he swears he didn't kill Josh but I know he did and*

"Why are there only fragments of what she wrote?"

Merrill sat back. "It has to do with Word 98 and how it caches things. You know what I mean?"

"Not really."

Merrill smiled at him, and Will knew he was about to get an explanation of how Merrill had gotten the pieces of her file open after she'd deleted them. This might take some time.

"You see," Merrill said, "this particular caching quirk can be picked up by opening a Word file with any text editor, such as Bare Bones' BBEdit. I actually took these fragments from one of her other files, the paper she wrote for English, you remember?"

"You mean Erin thought she'd deleted her files, but parts of them ended up in her English paper?"

"You've got it." An impish glint came into Merrill's eyes. "And what's cool about it is that this extraneous text is invisible when you're viewing the document in Word, but as soon as you use a text editor—bang!—it pops right out."

"Sounds dangerous."

"It is. Suppose you send a file to somebody over e-mail and they open it with a text editor and find your dirty laundry mixed in with a project proposal." Merrill giggled. "Shit, I love this stuff."

"I'm surprised a big company like Microsoft hasn't caught on to this yet."

"Oh, but they have."

Will should have known. For every problem there's a fix, and if anybody knew how to fix it, it was Merrill.

"Microsoft's Office 98 Unwanted Data Patch takes care of it, no problem. It squashes that 'ere bug."

"Good news." Will thought he might as well humor the man. Merrill had, after all, worked overtime on this.

"Actually, it's not only a problem with Word. It can happen with any application that uses Microsoft's OLE technology."

"What?"

"Object Linking and Embedding. It allows for applications to share data."

"Okay."

"Come on, Will. It's simple."

"How about we just blame Bill Gates?"

Merrill shrugged. "If that works for you."

Will asked, "Is that all there is? Nothing extraneous in other files?"

"This is all I could find."

Will stared at the screen and puzzled over Erin's words. What did they tell him? Mostly what he knew already. The words tumbled out of her about someone threatening her, her mother, and this same person she believed killed Josh.

"What do you suppose she means by 'Valhalla'?" Merrill asked.

"I have a feeling I should know."

"Isn't it where all the gods go when they die?" Merrill said. "Something like that?"

"I thought gods didn't die."

Merrill shrugged. "Should be easy to look up." Merrill got on the Internet and did a keyword search. "I was close," he said. The information on the screen revealed that Valhalla came from Scandinavian mythology and was the hall of Odin where the souls of the warrior heroes went after they died bravely.

But what did Valhalla have to do with Erin?

Will pictured Erin at her computer typing away madly, and his conversation with Kendra, describing her nightly antics, came back in a rush.

Erin hadn't been saying "Caballa" or "Willhalla." She'd been repeating "Valhalla."

Will sat in his truck outside the school, trying to figure out what to do next. Being armed with this piece of information about Valhalla didn't really do him any good, because he had no clue what it meant. Was Valhalla a real place? Was Erin speaking in code about something that only she and Josh knew about?

He returned to the house and placed a call to Malvina's office. He got her machine and left a message that he would meet her at the courthouse at ten the next morning and that there was no need to huddle; he trusted her to run the defense herself.

Soon after he left the message, Ray called. He had traced the numbers that Carmen had given him. Connecticut state police thought that the partial matched plates that might have been stolen.

Then Will sat in his leather chair and tried to imagine Erin writing late at night, recalled the words on the screen, the cryptic run-ons, and he was left with the strong feeling that Valhalla had to be a real place, that Erin wouldn't have found comfort and safety in an imagined world of Odin and his dead Scandinavian warriors. She had written in an agitated state, and the writing itself probably helped ground her, kept her from spinning out of control as she tried to work through her tormented thoughts.

So, if Valhalla actually existed, where was it? Will decided it had to be somewhere that she had known well, some place she probably shared with Josh, which meant it was probably somewhere on the Lloyd estate.

Will got to his feet and started pacing. Was it possible that the hunting camp was called Valhalla? It wasn't unusual, after all, to give hunting camps a name. His grandfather had called the camp in Quebec "Crosshairs." But "Valhalla" didn't quite fit. Besides, the camp had been empty.

He placed a phone call to Kathryn Lloyd right away. She had been the source, after all, of the explanation for the watches. He got the answering machine first, but Kathryn picked up when he explained who was calling and that it was an emergency.

"Is it Erin? Have you found her?" Kathryn asked.

"No."

"And now Laurie's missing, too?"

"You've heard about that?"

"It's been on the news. I've been praying for both of them." It occurred to Will that he hadn't turned on a TV in days. Of course the news would be full of the story.

Will asked Kathryn about Valhalla.

"My God! Where did you hear about that?"

Will fought to control his excitement. "So it's a real place?"

"Of course."

"Is it the hunting camp?"

"No. A fallout shelter."

"You're kidding."

"Jacko's father had it built in the fifties, you know, during the Red Scare. I don't think it's been used in years," Kathryn said.

"I'm not so sure about that."

Kathryn described where it was on the property, about a hundred yards due west of the house, near an oak tree. Was it possible that all this time Erin had been hiding there, a mere football field's length away when Will and Laurie had visited Candace? Will cursed himself for not taking a closer look at the property.

But he was certain now that Erin must be holed up in Valhalla. And maybe Laurie.

———

Will waited until evening. He wasn't sure if he was still being watched, but he knew he'd better take precautions just in case. He ate a bologna sandwich and plotted how best to get onto the Lloyd property without being seen.

About eight o'clock he drove his truck to Laurie's apartment house and let himself in with a key he found on a hook under the electric meter. Gloria the cat greeted him with angry meows. He had forgotten all about her. She must be starving.

After he fed her and scratched her ears, he rooted through Laurie's bureau and located the stainless-steel Smith & Wesson .359 she had retired from service a year previous. As he expected, the pistol was loaded. Will found a box of cartridges and stuffed his pockets. He had thought hard about this. He didn't like firearms, even though he knew how to use them, but he didn't know what he was going to walk into; he figured a pistol might come in handy.

He turned off the lights, parted the curtain, and studied the street. There was one parked car farther up. It looked like a Honda Civic. He made a mental note to keep an eye out for it in his rearview just in case. He glanced at his watch, then waited fifteen minutes before he made his move.

The extra set of keys for the Cherokee was in the cookie jar. Right where he imagined they'd be. Laurie was a creature of habit. Switching vehicles might not fool anybody, but he had to try what he could not to draw attention to himself.

He took a roundabout way to the Lloyd estate and doubled back on himself. The rearview was clean. It didn't occur to Will until he was on a side road approaching the estate from the south that he probably wouldn't be keeping his appointment for the probable-cause hearing in the morning.

Chapter 15

AFTER WILL TURNED OFF THE INTERSTATE, THE TRAFFIC thinned out. The back way beyond Ashland was dark, and the road wound sharply, the speed limit only thirty-five all the way to the Lloyd estate. There was a more direct route on a better highway, but Will figured he would more easily be able to spot someone following on the twisting road, especially given the slow speed limit.

He pulled off on several occasions and waited, his motor running, lights off, but it looked as if he had the road to himself. He had a passing thought that this careful dodging might be all folly, that someone might be waiting for him at the fallout shelter, but his instincts told him that whoever was out there didn't know about Valhalla and was still counting on him to lead the way to Erin.

He parked about a mile down from the Lloyd estate, just off the side of the road, so that if he didn't return, Laurie's Cherokee would be easily spotted. He made his way along the road edge, comforted by the bulge of the Smith & Wesson in his barn jacket.

The moon was full, the stars set against a clear, cold sky. He was thankful there was little wind. His eyes adjusted quickly to the darkness, and he soon reached an open field. The moon washed the landscape in silver, and the fence line extending to the north pointed a direct route to the estate.

He decided to approach the main house obliquely and climbed over the fence. He stopped when he came to a large pasture pine to check his bearings. The main house was dark except for the lights coming from the upstairs window of Candace's bedroom.

Will heard something behind him. He nudged his body closer to the tree. At first he thought the night had played tricks on him, but then he heard the light rustle again. He reached inside his coat pocket and gripped the Smith & Wesson. The rustling grew closer.

Will spun around the tree and leveled the pistol, and in the moonlight he could see a skunk sidling away from him. He pulled back to the pine and waited, listening to his heart thumping. He had to remain calm. He couldn't make a stupid mistake now.

When he settled himself, he made his way to the west, searching for the large oak Kathryn had described. He had little trouble spotting it. It was as if the tree had been grown purposely as a landmark for the fallout shelter.

As Will got closer, he could see a mound of earth next to the tree. He reasoned that the entrance was most likely from the top. Closer inspection revealed that the shelter had been built into the side of the hill.

Will recalled the fifties when these fallout shelters were in vogue—the national obsession with the Russians bombing the United States, the "duck and cover" drills in grade school, as if such efforts would do anything to stave off the effects of atomic warfare. He tried to imagine Jacko's father caught up in the scare, yet still retaining enough of a sense of irony to name his shelter "Valhalla," the hall of the dead heroes. Old Jackson Lloyd must have realized on some level that if the bombs fell, there would be little defense.

The door to the shelter was indeed on top of the mound,

but it took the beam from Will's flashlight to find it. The door—a small hatch, really—was camoflauged with dirt and weeds, but Will's spirits rose when he realized that there were signs that the earth around it had been recently disturbed.

He slowly opened the hatch and trained his light down what looked like a metal tube with a ladder attached. He called Erin's name. No response. He hesitated. Backing down the ladder was not the most strategic approach, but there seemed no other choice.

He tried to move quietly, but his boots clunked on the metal rungs, the tube acting as an echo chamber that magnified the sound. He looked down. It was so dark at the bottom that he had no idea how deep the thing went. It seemed to take forever to descend. He stopped, looked up once as he made his way down. The open hatch above revealed a tiny peephole to the sky.

When he finally reached the bottom, he had barely enough room to twist his body. He fumbled for what he imagined should be a door leading into the shelter. He reasoned that if he didn't need to use his flashlight, it would be harder for him to be seen. He found a doorknob and twisted it. The knob turned freely, but the door didn't give. Probably dead-bolted.

He leaned his face against the door. "Erin," he said. "It's Will Buchanan."

He waited. He imagined the door superthick by design, and he wondered if he could be heard at all. He threw his shoulder into it. It didn't budge.

He tried calling her name again, this time louder. His voice echoed through the tube. After that it didn't matter how much more noise he made. He'd surely drawn attention to himself by now, and there was little point in trying to remain quiet. He turned on his flashlight and studied the door.

If it wasn't steel, it was some compound equally strong. Old Jackson had spared no expense in constructing this thing. Will thought a moment. It occurred to him that since the shelter was built into a hillock, it didn't make sense that this was the only entrance. It would be too tough getting supplies down the hatch. There had to be another door, probably larger. It must be somewhere on the side of the hill.

Will started back up the ladder. The light from the moon shone faintly on the rungs. He was about halfway up when he heard the echoing slam of the hatch, and he was plunged into darkness.

He clung to the ladder. The pitch-black disoriented him, and he struggled to quell a rising panic. It took almost no time for the air to close in on him. He decided the best route was up. He would have to try to force open the hatch.

Deliberately and slowly, his hands clinging to the steel rungs, he made his way to the top, where, with one hand on the ladder, he raised the other above his head and pushed hard; to his surprise the hatch gave a bit. He removed the Smith & Wesson from his jacket and wedged the barrel between the hatch and the edge of the tube. A rush of cool air engulfed him.

But he knew he had only bought a little time. He couldn't hang there forever. Already he felt the pressure on his quads, and he had to shift his stance now and again to keep his legs from going numb, but this put stress on his arms and shoulders. The rungs bit into the soles of his boots.

Will didn't know how long he'd been on the ladder. His watch told him the time, but he hadn't checked it before descending. So far, since working his way back up to the top, he had clung to the ladder for at least a half hour. His muscles ached and burned. He decided he had no choice but to move back down before his strength gave out completely and he plummeted like a rock. There might not be enough room to sit at the bottom, but at least he could bend his knees.

He reached above his head and forced the pistol farther into the gap to widen it and allow as much fresh air in as possible. Satisfied that it was as open as it was going to get, Will slowly stepped back down again.

The air stank of mildewed cement. At the bottom he slumped against the door. He told himself to get up, but his muscles refused. He began to feel light-headed breathing in the foul air.

He had a passing thought of the pistol lodged between the hatch and the edge of the tank, and he almost laughed out loud. He imagined a reporter asking, "And did you have to use the Smith & Wesson?" And his smug reply: "Yes. They make great wedges."

Suddenly the door he'd been leaning against opened, and he tumbled across the threshold into a darkened room. He immediately felt a rush of air, sucked it in, then coughed.

Someone spoke. "Hello, Will."

It was a voice he'd never heard before.

―――――

It took a few moments for Will to recover. He rose up on his hands and scanned the dimly lit room. In the corner a figure sat on a lower bunk, head in hands, identity lost in shadow.

The voice spoke again. It came from the corner of the room opposite the bunk. "It took you long enough to find her."

"Who are you?"

"I'm surprised you haven't guessed."

Will got to his feet. He hobbled toward the bunk on stiff legs. He touched the shoulder of the sitting figure. "Erin?" he said.

She didn't respond at first. Then Will took hold of her hand. His touch seemed to break her out of a trance. She stood and threw her arms around him. A shudder ran through her body.

"Now, that makes a nice picture," the voice said.

Erin felt stiff in his arms. He recalled that day out on the woodlot when she wouldn't let him go. It was the same fierce embrace. She must be scared out of her wits.

"Get away from her," the voice said.

"Let go, Erin." Will tried to unclasp her arms.

"Erin. Sit down," the voice said.

Immediately the strength ebbed out of Erin. She meekly assumed her position on the bunk again and said nothing.

"Step closer," the voice said.

Will complied. He strained his eyes as he walked toward the corner, trying to make out who was speaking, but all he could see was a shadowy outline.

"Empty your pockets," the voice said. "Slowly."

Will took out loose change and a pocketknife and placed them on a table in the center of the room. Then his wallet and handkerchief.

"That's all?"

Will's eyes had adjusted to the light enough so he could tell that the voice was coming from behind shelves that looked as if they had cans and bottles on them. "Show yourself," Will said.

"In due time. You have no weapon?"

"That's all I've got." Will gestured toward the table. "You've been following me, haven't you."

"Yes."

"You kept waiting for me to lead you to Erin." Will took a step toward him.

"Stay where you are."

Will backed off.

"Like I said. It took you long enough," the voice said.

"But how did you do it?"

"You mean tonight?"

So there were other times. "You followed me to the hunting lodge?"

"Yes. You're pretty hard to track down, I'll give you that."

Will moved closer, straining his eyes. The one responsible for everything, for Josh's murder and most likely Erin's rape, was standing not five feet from him. But who was he? "And tonight?" Will asked. "What was my mistake?"

"I eventually caught on where you were going. I figured it would take some time for you to get to the estate with all your backtracking, so I took the faster route."

At least Will felt vindication that his hunch had been right about being followed, but it made him angry to think that this guy had guessed where he was going. Here he had spent all that time dodging phantoms while his stalker had simply circled around and waited for him.

"I knew you'd eventually figure out where Erin was," the voice said. "All I had to do was be patient."

"Where's Laurie?"

"I don't know what you're talking about." He hesitated. "Now turn around."

"What happens next?"

"I said turn around."

Will slowly shifted back to Erin—then felt a dull thud on the back of his head. His legs buckled, and he fell to the floor.

———

When he regained consciousness, Erin was sitting on the floor watching him. He sat up and rubbed the back of his head. "God, what did he hit me with?"

"Just his hand, I think," Erin said.

"You're kidding." Will felt for blood but, from what he could tell, there was no open wound.

"He knows all about that stuff from the service. How to knock people out. He was a SEAL, you know."

The story sounded familiar. Then his conversation with Laurie came back to him. "A SEAL? Erin. This man isn't your father, is he?"

"Yes." She slowly began to rock her body. "And he can kill people with his bare hands, do you know that? At least that's what he says. Can kill people with his bare hands."

Will grabbed her shoulders to keep her from rocking. "Erin. Slow down."

"But I fooled him. I ran away, and he didn't know where I was. I fooled him, and he didn't know."

Will slowly helped her up and led her back to the bunk. "You need to lie down, Erin."

She threw her arms around him again and spoke in his ear. "I'm so sorry. So sorry. I didn't mean to hurt you. You've been so good to me."

Will let her cry. How long had she been down in this hole by herself? Probably since running away from the rape crisis center. All that time living in paralyzing fear that her father would somehow find where she was. And Will had led him to her.

He tried to soothe Erin's panic with soft words. He didn't know how long he'd held her in his arms, but it took some time for her to relax enough for him to urge her to lie back down on the bunk. He covered her with a blanket.

"Don't leave me," she said. "Please don't leave me."

He brushed the hair off her forehead. "I'm not going anywhere."

"I'm so cold."

Will rubbed her shoulders briskly. "Try to close your eyes."

"I can't sleep. I'm so sorry. I was a bad girl. He says I'm a bad girl, and I am. I know I am."

Will stood, his back aching from bending over the bunk, and walked toward the center of the room.

"Where are you going?" she asked.

"Is there a chair down here? I need to sit."

"There's a box near the shelves."

Will found it and placed it next to the bunk. "See? I'm here, Erin." He sat on the box. "I'm not going anywhere."

"I need to tell you things," Erin said.

"I know. But not now." He placed a hand on her back.

"He made me do that stuff. I didn't want to. He made me."

"Erin, relax. Get some sleep."

Will kept his hand on her, and gradually he could feel her breathing slowing down. She soon settled and appeared to drift off; he carefully removed his hand.

He had a pounding headache from the blow, and he rubbed the back of his neck to relieve the stiffness. He suddenly felt tired and allowed himself a few minutes to lean on the edge of the bunk and rest his head on his arms.

But the discovery of who had been behind all this kept him wide awake. Why had Harold Wickham put his daughter through such torture? And where had he gone off to? Will knew that the answers would emerge soon, but right now he had a job to do. He had to figure a way to get out.

He stretched his muscles and got up. He headed for the shelves, where he found candles and matches along with canned fruits and vegetables. He struck a match and watched as the flame rose.

He lit a candle and held it high, trying to locate the source of ventilation. Near the rear of the shelter, he found a shaft big enough for a man to fit into, and it suddenly came clear how Harold Wickham had been able to waylay him: After closing the hatch on Will and leaving him suspended on the ladder, Wickham had probably made his entrance through the shaft by rope, no doubt scaring the wits out of Erin in the process.

Will held the candle as high up the shaft as he could. The shaft was angled into the earth, a fairly easy descent for Wickham. Going up it, though, without the aid of a rope, would be another story, and Will doubted there would be enough purchase on the slick sides for him to make it all the way to the top. Perhaps he could fashion something on his boots, though, that would help him stick.

If he could just get to the top, he could retrieve the Smith & Wesson and surprise Wickham on his return. All this depended, of course, on Wickham's not having noticed the pistol wedged in the hatch as he left. But even if Wickham had retrieved it, Will would still have surprise on his side.

He thought of Laurie again. Was Wickham lying when he said he had no idea what Will was talking about? Will guessed that it *was* a lie, and Wickham knew exactly where she was.

Will took his candle and investigated behind the shelves. As he suspected, there was a door, one that must originally have been used to supply the shelter. Just to make sure, he tried it. A strong push revealed that the door gave slightly at the top and bottom—probably latched from the center. Will doubted he could break it open. The best chance remained in going up the shaft.

He searched the shelves again for something he might be able to rub on the bottom of his boots, and the best he could come up with was a can of maple syrup. He brought it down and shook it—no liquid movement at all. The syrup was no doubt caramelized. Perhaps if he heated it up? It would take more heat than one candle could supply, though, and his shoulders dropped in disappointment. Maybe there was a stove somewhere.

But he could find nothing like a stove. Wickham had even remembered to take Will's pocketknife, so he didn't have anything to scrape out the hardened syrup. At least Wickham had had the decency to leave Will's spare change on the table.

He went back to the shaft. He had to try going up the thing. He bent his long frame inside and pressed his back against the metal edge. He lifted his right leg and pushed hard against the opposite side. He slid his back up along the shaft and tried to lift his left leg, but as soon as he did, he lost the grip of his boot. He fell unceremoniously to the floor. He tried it again, and the same thing happened.

The noise generated from this fruitless exercise awakened Erin. "Mr. Buchanan! Where are you?"

"I'm here, Erin."

"Why did you leave me?"

Will brushed himself off and headed back to her bunk. She was sitting up. "It's okay. I haven't gone anywhere," he said. He explained what he'd been doing.

"Do you want me to try?" she asked.

"It's too dangerous. That shaft is pretty high."

"You can at least let me try it. I'm a lot smaller than you are and I'm pretty strong."

What did he have to lose? "Okay. I'll spot you."

But Erin had as much trouble as Will. The problem wasn't getting started, but sustaining the right pressure between the feet and back. Will's rock-climbing experience had come in handy for technique—what climbers call "chimneys," where two opposing rock faces are positioned tightly together and progress is made by sliding the shoulders while alternatively pushing the feet, is something Will had done quite a bit of in his youth.

Will coached her, but the metal was just too slick for Erin to maintain enough counterforce pressure to proceed upward. He suggested that she stack her feet in a T configuration, so that one foot was placed parallel to one side of the shaft while the other was positioned perpendicular to it, jammed between the first foot and the opposite wall. This seemed to work the best, but the strenuous effort soon took its toll, and Erin's muscles gave out. In one last-ditch attempt, Will tried to sneak in underneath her and push her up as far as his arms would reach to see if the shaft made a turn or the sides weren't as slick, but she lost her balance and came tumbling down on top of him.

They both sat on the floor recovering from their efforts. Will stared hard at the shaft. There must be a way to get up the thing. If he could find something long, like a pole or a piece of wood, he might be able to shove it up and at least see where the bends were. It bothered him that he couldn't see light from the top.

He was about to go searching when the back door suddenly flew open and Harold Wickam reentered the room. Erin ran quickly to the bunk and buried her head in the pillow.

"Now, what have you two been up to?" Wickham asked, seeing Will at the shaft. "You haven't been trying to escape, have you?"

It took a moment for Will to realize that Wickham wasn't alone, and his spirits lifted when he recognized the blindfolded figure Wickham shoved into the room as Laurie.

Chapter 16

WILL RUSHED TO LAURIE. HE HELPED HER TO HER FEET and took her into his arms. Her hands were bound behind her, her face streaked with dirt. From behind them the door slammed, and a hasp closed and locked. Harold Wickham had disappeared as quickly as he'd arrived.

"Untie me," Laurie said.

"Are you okay?"

"I think so."

Erin lifted her head from the pillow. "Aunt Laurie?"

"Erin? Oh, my God. You're alive!" She rushed toward her niece and embraced her, stroked her hair and held her close. "I never thought I'd see you again," she said.

"He didn't hurt you, did he?" Erin asked.

"I'm fine." Laurie looked around the room. "Where are we?"

"Valhalla," Will said.

"What?"

"It's an old fallout shelter," Erin said. "Josh and I used to play in here when we were kids."

Laurie turned to Will. "Think we can get out of here?"

"I don't know. We were trying to get up the ventilation shaft when you made your entrance."

"We've got to get out," Laurie said. She looked at Erin. "I don't know what your father's up to."

"I know what he's up to," Erin said.

Will paused. Of course she did. "Erin, I'm sure you can fill us in on a lot, but we've got to concentrate on escaping from here. Do you know of another way out? If you played here as kids, you must have been able to break into the place."

"No. Josh always stole the key. We liked to come down that long ladder."

"There's no other entrance, no other airway?" Laurie prompted.

"I don't think so," Erin said.

Above their heads a metallic banging noise. Will said, "Sounds like Harold's making sure we don't get out through the shaft."

"He's capping it," Laurie said.

"We'll suffocate!" Erin said.

Will gently placed his hand on her arm. "I don't think so. He'll make sure enough air gets in."

"You don't know that," Erin insisted

"He wants us alive, at least for now," Will said. "He'll be back for us."

"I'm so sorry," Erin said, her eyes welling with tears. "This is my fault. I didn't mean to be bad. He says I'm bad, and he's right. I shouldn't have loved Josh. It was evil. He's my father and . . ."

The words continued to spill out of her in a rush. Her legs grew weak, and Laurie helped her back to her bunk. How could any man have done this to his daughter? Harold Wickham was a monster.

While Laurie comforted Erin, Will decided to check the room thoroughly to see if he'd overlooked any possibility of escape. The place had been built so long ago, there might be a weak spot somewhere, where the earth had broken through. The ventilation shaft was larger than the flue of a freestanding fireplace and must have originally been filtered somehow for atomic particles, that system obviously long ago abandoned. There *was* airflow in the room, which meant that exchange was happening, but how was the air escaping?

Will carried a candle with him, but he relied more on touch as he ran his hand along the walls of the structure. It took him about an hour to cover the whole room, and his search yielded nothing but hard cement. It was only when he stepped up onto the table and focused the candle on the ceiling that he saw the bore holes. There was not just one exit for the air but several, each about a foot in diameter.

It was an ingenious design, practical and functional. Most shelters built during the Red Scare were cramped and dank and would probably be obliterated in the first flash. But this palatial ark just might have weathered it. Jackson Lloyd senior had simply built the strongest brick shithouse in the Western Hemisphere.

As Will worked his hands along the wall's surface, he thought hard about what he would do when Wickham came back for them. Erin could tell them a few things, he was sure, but he didn't know if in her current state she would be capable of yielding much information without breaking down. Twice Erin had gotten close to talking about her father, and twice she'd been reduced to a babbling state. There were flashes of coherence, though, as when she'd helped Will try to escape up the ventilation shaft. Now perhaps, with Laurie's help, she could be encouraged to open up.

Laurie left Erin's bedside and approached Will in the center of the room. He stepped down from the table.

"She asleep?" Will asked.

"Yes. I think so."

"The minute she starts talking about her father, she falls into blithering, then shuts down."

"What has she told you?" Laurie asked.

"Not much." Will searched the shelves and found a dusty can of peaches. He hefted the can. "Now all we need to do is find a way to open it."

Laurie sat on the bench. "How did you know to look for Erin here?"

Will placed the can of peaches on the table, sat on the opposite bench, and told his story.

"So Merrill Fogarty turned out to be the key," Laurie said.

"Yes, we have him to thank for discovering Erin's hiding place. I thought maybe I'd find you here, too."

"Wickham took me to his camper after he grabbed me."

"The one he moved from the Chocorua site?"

She nodded.

"Where did he grab you?"

"About five miles from the campground, on the road to Conway. He had the hood up on his truck, and I figured he needed assistance." She paused. "It was stupid. I should have known better."

"I don't know why. I mean, how were you to know who he was?"

"I guess I was getting too close, and it was worth kidnapping me until he could find Erin."

"Yeah. I did a good job of leading him here."

"Don't blame yourself."

"But I do."

"You forced his hand, look at it that way."

Will suddenly sat forward. "Wait a minute," he said. "I just thought of something."

"You're going to break down the walls with your bare hands?"

"No. Listen. I've been focused so much on escape. . . . What if we locked Wickham out?"

"What good would that do?"

"Think about it. As long as we're in here, we're safe. He can't get to us."

"But we have no food, no water."

"We could last a few days."

"I don't know. I haven't eaten in two days already."

Will stared at the can of peaches. "We've got to find a way to get this damn can open."

"Do you really think locking him out would work?"

"The key is Kathryn. She knows I called about Valhalla. I'm hoping she'll sound the alarm."

"Then it might be worth a shot."

"Especially since I'll be missing my hearing. With any luck it will make the news."

"You missed your probable-cause hearing?"

"Well, it's your fault. If you didn't go and get yourself kidnapped, I would have kept my schedule."

Laurie shook her head but said nothing.

"How long do you think we have before Harold comes back?"

"I don't know. He said something about having to move vehicles."

"Must be switching locations."

"The cruiser and camper, probably. My guess is he's looking for a place to hide them."

"And your Cherokee," Will said.

"What?"

Will told her about swapping cars.

"Super. You could have at least used your truck."

"Oh. You mean there's no great loss if anything happened to it?"

"It would be a blessing."

"Hey, watch it."

"My Cherokee? You had to take my Cherokee?"

"I told you, I was trying to get him off my tail."

"Damn it, Will. If anything happens to it . . ."

"I'll buy you a new one."

"Sure you will."

"God, Laurie. Listen to yourself. We're in deep shit here, and you're worried about your damn car!"

She paused. "You're right." She was quiet for a moment. "How much time do you think we have before he comes back?"

"I don't know. I assume he hasn't gotten much rest either. He might have to take a break before he deals with us."

Laurie looked at the can of peaches on the table. "Think you can get that thing open?"

———

Will followed through on his plan to lock out Harold Wickham. The doors were easily dead-bolted from the inside. If there'd been a nuclear war, Jackson Lloyd senior had made sure that nobody else would come busting into the shelter.

But as Will shoved the bolts into the slides, he wondered why the doors could be locked from the outside as well, and then it occurred to him that the exterior locks must have been an added feature, most likely there to keep peacetime vandals away.

Erin soon stirred. Laurie went to her and sat on the box

next to the bed. Will could hear them talking in low voices as he tried smashing the can of peaches several times against the concrete wall. He had no idea how long the can had been down there, but the thought of the peaches stirred his stomach and made him work harder to open it.

The can soon ruptured at the seam where the lid meets the top, and he used a coin to wedge into the opening. He twisted the coin a few times and eventually had space to insert a finger, padded with his handkerchief. He pulled up on the lid, careful not to cut himself, but the metal wouldn't budge. He removed his finger, tipped the can to his mouth, and drank the sweet syrup. He brought the canned peaches to Laurie.

"Want a swig?" he asked. "It's really good."

"You got it open?"

"Partway."

He handed the can to Laurie, who in turn held it out for Erin. "Drink some. You'll feel better."

Erin sat up and tipped the can to her mouth.

Will asked Erin, "How are you feeling?"

"Okay, I guess." She drank again. "Hmm."

"Tastes good?" Will asked.

"I'm starving."

"Drink some more," Laurie said.

"I don't want to take the whole thing." Erin handed the can back to Laurie. "You haven't had any."

Laurie brushed away her hand. "I don't like peaches," she said.

"Come on, Aunt Laurie. I know that's not true."

"How long have you been down in this hole?" Will said.

"Since I ran away from the rape crisis center."

"But what have you been doing for food?" Laurie asked.

"I'd go into the big house late at night through a window and rob the kitchen. Robert doesn't hear too well anymore."

"But he must have noticed the food disappearing," Will said.

"Maybe, but he never caught on I was in the shelter."

"Are you sure?" Laurie asked.

"Nobody knows I'm here except you." She paused. "And my father, of course. You're not going to leave me, are you?"

"Where would we go?" Laurie said.

Erin didn't say anything. She let her head drop to the pillow, and Will wondered if she was going to nod off to sleep again. Her shutting down so quickly was most likely a sign of the deep stress she was under.

"We're certainly not going anywhere right now," Will said. "You should know that we have a plan to keep your father away from you."

"A plan?"

"We've locked all the doors. He won't be able to get in."

This seemed to energize Erin, and she sat up again. "But that won't keep him out. I had the doors locked, too, and he still got in." Another tremor ran through her body, and Laurie coaxed her to lie back and told her to relax. "The difference is that we're here now," she said. "You're not alone."

"Don't let him hurt me again, Aunt Laurie! Please don't let him hurt me!"

"No one's going to hurt you," Will said.

Erin's eyes suddenly fixed on Will. "I'm sorry, Mr. Buchanan. You must think I'm really evil."

"Go back to sleep," Will said.

"No, I don't want to. I need to talk about it."

Laurie said, "But you need to rest, too."

"My father killed Josh."

"We know that," Laurie said.

"He was waiting for me at school when I got back from Kathryn's."

"And he was the one you were seeing when you were past in-dorm time," Will said.

"Yes. My father kept trying to convince me to go with him. He said we were going to pick up my mom and be a family again. It was God's will."

"Why didn't he just kidnap you?"

"He told me he was waiting for the commotion over Josh's death to calm down. Then we were going to make our escape. But I think he also wanted to persuade me to go with him on my own. He was real nice about it in the beginning, telling me how much he loved me and that he was saving me from a sinful life, but . . ."

"When you refused, it turned ugly," Will said.

"That night I showed up at your place was right after he had lost it. I tried to fight him off."

Will hesitated. "Did your father rape you, Erin?"

It took her a while to answer. "I told him I would never go with him. We screamed at each other. He made me take off all my clothes. Then he beat me. He bruised me down there, but he didn't penetrate me." She paused. "When he gave me back my underpants to put on, they were moist. I think he ejaculated into them."

"To make it look like a rape," Will said.

"But only after he realized he had stepped over the line by

beating me so hard. I think he had to do something about how bad he felt. He had never hit me like that before, and I guess it frightened him."

There was no doubt in Will's mind that Wickham had realized that by the time the DNA tests were in and Will was cleared, Wickham and Erin would be long gone.

"So he transferred his guilt to me."

Erin looked off into space. "Something like that, I guess. Who knows what was going through his mind? All I know is he kept saying I had to report you, and that's when he told me he would kill my mom if I didn't do what he said. I'm sorry, Mr. Buchanan—I was just so scared."

Laurie said, "That's enough for now, Will."

"No. It's all right." Erin sat up again. "I need to tell you both what I know."

Will pressed on. "And was it also his idea for you come on to me, Erin? To spread those rumors about our being lovers?"

Erin looked up at him, her eyes moist. "No. I did that on my own. I guess I knew I needed someone to help me fight him, and it was the only way I could think of. You have to understand, Mr. Buchanan, I was desperate. I just thought if I could get you to be mine—in some way, I wasn't sure how— you would protect me."

"Why didn't you just ask for my help?"

"Because I was terrified! He threatened to hurt me more if I told anyone about him." Erin sobbed. "And . . . and . . . my mom."

Laurie held Erin close. "Will, for God's sake."

"Just one more thing, Erin. Did your father mention why he was coming back for you at this time? Why now?"

Erin wiped her eyes with her sleeve. "I think he'd been

watching me for years. And when he found out that Josh and I were lovers, he saw that as the ultimate corruption of his family and his religion."

"And so your father felt he had to kill Josh. To save you from a life of sin?"

She looked up at Will. "He told me he watched us that day in the woods when we went to Zealand Falls, Mr. Buchanan. Josh and I had just missed each other so much. . . ."

"I'm afraid I was there, too," Will said.

"What?"

"I was out looking for a place to camp and stumbled on you two."

"Oh, my God! I'm so sorry!" She started crying again.

Will studied Erin. He could just imagine what Wickham had thought when he discovered that his daughter was having an affair with the son of the man who'd stolen his wife away from him. And to actually catch them in the act—it must have been too much for Wickham to deal with. "I'm sorry, Erin. This is really the last question, I promise," he said. "What about the money? The twenty-five thousand."

"I stole it from him," she said. "He's got a fortune stashed in his camper. I couldn't let you stay in jail, Mr. Buchanan!"

Will was about to reply when there was a pounding on the door.

Chapter 17

WILL HELD UP HIS HAND. "STAY HERE," HE SAID. HE approached the steel door and listened. More muffled pounding. The dead bolt rattled, a slight tremor, as Wickham pushed and thumped. With his ear to the door, Will could barely make out his faint cursing. Then there was silence.

"Is he gone?" Laurie asked.

"I think so." Will came back to the bed and found Erin curled up, staring into space.

Laurie placed her hand on her shoulder. "It's all right," she said. "Your father's not going to get in here."

Erin's eyes were blank and unmoving.

Laurie slowly removed her hand. She stood, took Will's arm, and led him away from the bed. "We've got to get her out of here."

"I know."

"What's Wickham's next move?"

"He'll be back. He won't give up that easily."

"I don't like this. Making him mad probably wasn't the best idea."

"You want to just open the door and let him in?"

"Maybe we can talk him out of it."

"Sure. He sounds like a reasonable guy."

Laurie started to say something, then shook her head. "I'm just worried about Erin."

Will held Laurie. "We've at least bought some time," he said.

"You're sure you told Kathryn where you were going?"

"She knows."

Laurie held him at arm's length. "But did you actually say she should call the police if you didn't show?"

"No. I didn't actually say that to her." With that admission, even in the faint light, he could tell that the color had drained from her face.

"We don't have a chance, do we," she said.

"As long as we have time, we do."

But how much time did they have? And what sort of chance? Perhaps all he'd accomplished by locking out Wickham was a delay of the inevitable. But he couldn't think about that.

Laurie returned to the bed, sat on the edge, and talked softly to Erin, who still appeared lost somewhere.

With the air shaft the only open entrance left, Will decided it was best to stand guard. But if Wickham attempted to come down it again, would he be ready for him? He considered his options. Perhaps if he blocked the shaft with the table, just moved it into place so that air could still circulate underneath, it would at least make it harder for Wickham to enter the room.

The table was heavy. Will had trouble budging it at first, but he was able to skooch it a little at a time by shifting its corners. Finally he had it in place. If Wickham came down after them, he would get tangled up in the crosspiece that ran along the bottom of the table, and Will would have a better chance of disarming him. While this moving project was going on, Laurie had looked up once, eyed him curiously, but said nothing.

It occurred to Will he must have appeared foolish, but it felt good to at least do something.

He moved the benches over next to the shaft and arranged them to further confound Wickham's imagined entrance.

He suddenly felt drained and sat down on the end of one of benches, placed his arms on the table, and rested his head. He closed his eyes, not a good idea. He felt light-headed from exhaustion and lack of sleep, and there was a buzzing in his ears. He grabbed the edges of the table to steady himself. He forced his eyes open, and the room gradually stopped moving.

He was about to search again for something he might possibly have overlooked to use as a weapon when he heard noises from above. "Wickham's back!" he shouted. "Right above us!"

"Is he coming down the shaft?" Laurie asked.

"I don't hear him yet," he said. "Get me that can of peaches, will you?"

Laurie brought it to him. "You're going to kill him with a can of peaches?"

"Just give it to me. What else—"

But before Will could finish the sentence, a rattling came from inside the shaft and grew louder as they listened—then the shatter of glass against the table, followed by a flash of fire. In an instant the table was engulfed in flames. It was a gasoline bomb, a Molotov cocktail. The heat immediately drove Will and Laurie back into the center of the room.

"Get a blanket!" he shouted.

Laurie ran toward Erin, who was sitting up, her eyes wide in the light of the flames. In the time it took for Laurie to grab the blanket, another incendiary careened down the shaft and exploded at Will's feet. He jumped back, but too late. His pant leg flared up like a torch.

Erin screamed.

Laurie dove for Will's leg with the blanket and smothered the flames. Her efforts controlled the damage, but Will could still feel the sear on his leg.

He grabbed the blanket out of Laurie's hands and began beating at the fire that had all but consumed the table, but his efforts were futile; the smoke began to envelop the room. In such close quarters, Will knew it would take little time for them to be overwhelmed. He coughed and ran for Erin. He took hold of her arms and urged her to the floor.

"Crawl to the door!" he shouted. He breathed in smoke and again coughed hard. He felt Laurie's hand on his butt, pushing him toward the door.

They had to feel their way now, the smoke thickening, the visibility all but blocked. Will dropped from his knees to his belly and crawled the remaining distance. Laurie forced Erin closer to the floor and followed Will's lead.

When Will reached the door, he worked himself up its length and undid the bolt just as Laurie struggled with the bottom latch.

He pushed, and the door sprang open.

Will shoved Erin and Laurie ahead, then tumbled into the dark. The shock of the clean, cold air forced a sharp gasp that ripped at his lungs.

———

They were met by a bright light shining in their faces. Wickham's voice boomed from behind it. "Don't try anything."

Will struggled to his feet, his breathing sharp and labored. When he stepped to the side of the light, he could see Wickham's body in shadow. He was holding a gun pointed directly at Laurie.

"You're getting me irritated, Buchanan," Wickham said, his voice calm. "You try any more tricks and Laurie dies first. You'll have the pleasure of watching."

Will raised his hands. "No more tricks."

Laurie held Erin close. "Let her go," she said.

"And you can keep quiet, too."

"People know we're here," Laurie persisted.

"I said shut up!" Wickham let the beam of his flashlight fall to the ground. "Now I want you to march toward the house, one behind the other, like good little soldiers." He paused. "You're in the lead, Will."

Will started walking. The sky was striated with clouds, just a few stars visible. There had been a recent light snowfall since he'd been imprisoned in the fallout shelter, and if it hadn't been for the circumstances, he would have taken pleasure from the simple act of stretching his legs and feeling his lungs settle to a normal breathing process. But the walking was difficult because his leg still felt on fire.

He couldn't get his mind off the pistol that he imagined remained wedged in the hatch door, and he ignored the pain in his leg, preoccupying himself with how he could he get at it.

Behind them the fire lit the sky. There was hope there, too. Wickham was taking a chance that someone wouldn't see it, but he probably also knew the chance was slim; the Lloyd estate was so isolated, the fire most likely wouldn't be visible from any traveled road.

As the house came into closer view, Will wondered about Candace and Robert. Surely they would have noticed the fire. They might have called the cops. But were they still alive? There would be little doubt that Wickham had thought of these contingencies before settling on the idea of torching the shelter.

Wickham prodded them toward the central garage, an impressive building with eight bays. At his urging, Will opened a side door and entered the garage. Wickham turned on the lights.

In the bay closest to the side door, Laurie's cruiser was parked, and next to it was her Cherokee. There were other vehicles down the rows, but from where Will was standing, he couldn't make them out. "What now?" he said.

"In due time."

"You'd better have a pretty good plan," Will said. "It won't take long for people to realize we're missing."

"I appreciate your concern, Will."

Laurie spoke suddenly. "Give it up, Harold. Let us go."

Wickham interrupted her. "Everybody just keep quiet," he said. "You don't think I've got a plan? You don't think this has all been worked out?"

"I think it got bigger than you thought it would," Will said.

"It doesn't matter how big it got. Erin is mine now. She's back where she needs to be. Don't you people get it?"

"No," Will said. He looked Wickham directly in the eyes. "Enlighten me." It occurred to him that until this point he'd never seen the man up close, that the harsh light in the garage now afforded the only opportunity to examine Erin's father out of shadow. Wickham's face was pocked and stubbled with several days' growth, and the eyes, hard and brooding, revealed conviction born of unwavering intent, a crazed look that sent a shiver through Will.

Wickham did not back away from Will's gaze. "It won't matter soon anyway," he said.

The condescension in Wickham's voice irritated Will, and he decided to push the man. "Try me."

"You are going to die," Wickham said. "I suppose you can understand that much."

"And you're going to kill me?"

"Well, let's just say you're going to have an accident."

"You mean like Josh had an accident?"

"Yes, that was unfortunate." Wickham turned away suddenly and looked at Erin. "It had to be done for my daughter's sake."

Erin didn't look at her father. She resisted silently by stiffening her arms, but Wickham would not let her go.

"Tell me," Will said, "did Jackson Lloyd also have an accident?"

"I think you know the answer to that. He was the one who started this whole thing."

"Because he was a wife stealer?"

"I've done enough talking."

"What's the matter, Harold? Afraid of the truth?"

Wickham sighed. "No. I just find it a waste of time explaining what you'll never understand."

"It was your wife that ran away from you, Harold," Will said. "She did it because she wanted to save herself and her daughter. Jacko just protected her from you. He didn't deserve to die."

"Of course he did." Wickham paused. "He took everything I loved. He took my wife and destroyed her. She can't even walk about the house now without help. And he wrecked his own family in the process. If anyone deserved to die, it was Jacko."

"And have you become God, Harold? Deciding who should live and die?"

He smirked. "I'm just following God's will. And perhaps any man who wears such an expensive watch deserves to die."

Will stared at Wickham for a moment without saying anything. Wickham's smile broadened as he waited for Will's reaction. It had been a while since Will had even thought of the Rolex, but now he saw clearly how Jackson Lloyd's pricey watch had made its way to Zealand Falls.

"You stole Jacko's Rolex after you killed him," Will said.

"A trophy. A mere reminder of the obscenity of his life. Every time I looked at my wrist, I knew I had done the right thing."

"When Josh fought with you above the falls, he clutched at anything to keep his balance, and his hand just happened to grab at your wrist."

"He put up a hell of a fight, I'll give him that."

"That's why the band was broken at the link."

"It held for a while. I thought he was going to pull me over."

Erin suddenly screamed, a sharp-edged wail that echoed stridently in the enclosed garage, and it was so unexpected that Wickham drew back abruptly, like he had been snake-bit. Laurie pulled Erin close.

Wickham looked offended. "Now look at what you've done," he said. "You've made her upset."

"*I've* made her upset?" Will said.

"All right. That's enough." He turned away from Will and faced Laurie. "On that bench at the rear of the garage is some rope. I'd like you to get it for me."

Laurie stiffened. "Get it yourself," she said.

Wickham's hand shot out swiftly, and he cuffed her face. Will rose to defend her and was met by a swift uppercut to his gut that doubled him over—then a stiff, right cross that brought him to the floor.

It happened so quickly Will had the sense that Wickham's fist had appeared out of nowhere, as if aided by the invisible hand of divine intervention.

By the time Will got to his feet, Wickham had drawn his pistol. It was Laurie's Smith & Wesson. Will's heart sank. It wasn't so much that he'd thought of a plan to retrieve it as it was something that had always represented hope—Wickham didn't overlook much.

"Turn around," Wickham said.

Will complied.

"Now I'm going to ask you again to get that rope for me."

Will could hear Laurie moving toward the bench.

Wickham said, "I want you to tie Will's hands behind him. I want you to tie him up real good."

When Laurie was finished, Wickham tested the knots. He sat Will down on the floor. "Now his feet," he said. The cement floor was hard and cold.

Once Will was trussed up, Wickham did the same for Laurie. "You two shouldn't be able to cause much damage now," he said. He reached out and touched Erin's hair. "Come on, sweetie. Let's go see your mother."

AFTER THEY LEFT, WILL ROLLED ONTO HIS SIDE AND faced Laurie. "What's your take on that?"

"On what?"

"Erin. It's like she suddenly changed from victim to cat woman."

"She's manic, Will. I can't imagine what she's going through."

"But did you see when the change happened?" Will said. "Right after Harold described how Josh fought him above the falls—it was like that scream woke her up."

Laurie frowned. "What do you think he's doing now?"

"I wouldn't worry about Candace, Laurie. If Harold hasn't hurt her by now, I don't think he's going to."

"I wish I could be sure."

"Trust me. He has no need to hurt her. She's certainly not going to run out for help, and I'm sure he's cut the phone lines by now."

"We've got to free ourselves."

"What kind of knot did you use on me?"

"Just a square knot."

Will turned his back to her. "This shouldn't be too hard if you can find the ends."

They lay back to back, Laurie's hands positioned a little above his. "I can't free my hands up enough to work the knot," she said.

"Keep trying."

Laurie fumbled with the rope for a good fifteen minutes, and then they switched roles. Will thought he might be making progress on her knot, but the rope was too stiff, and he couldn't get enough leverage to force the ends.

"We need to try something else," he said. "You know, I think our only hope here is Erin."

"What can she do? The poor kid is traumatized."

"Up until a few hours ago, I would have agreed, but the way she screamed at him makes me think she's about had enough. Maybe she's found the guts that helped her run away from him in the first place."

"You sure that just isn't wishful thinking?"

Will considered. "I don't know. We'll be able to tell pretty quickly when they get back. In the meantime maybe we can find something sharp to work at these ropes."

"What do you suppose is happening?"

"Laurie, will you stop torturing yourself? They're having a family discussion. You heard the man."

"Do you really think Wickham's got a plan?"

"He's too careful not to have one," Will said. "It's pretty clever how he's been able to keep himself out of suspicion by controlling his appearances. I mean, I'm sure we've been reported missing, but I'd be surprised if Wickham's even a suspect in any of this."

"I'm hoping Ray will figure it out."

"But how? All he's got is the name the camper was registered under. He has a partial plate from Connecticut that's no doubt stolen. What else has he got?"

"Speaking of which," Laurie said, "where do you suppose the camper is?"

"Parked somewhere. It's part of his plan."

"And we're probably not."

"That's right. We need to be taken care of."

Laurie lay quiet a few moments. "I'm sorry, Will."

"About what?"

"Everything."

"We're going to get out of this, Laurie. So don't start—"

"I should have trusted you more," she said. "I know that now. I needed to let you into my life. If it hadn't been for—"

"Laurie, will you shut up? We can talk forever once we get out of here. Right now we need to focus on how we can get our hands untied."

———

Will thought he might try his luck with freeing the rope around Laurie's legs, but he ran into the same difficulty of not being able to get leverage.

"It's no good," she said. "Don't waste your energy."

"I've got to do something."

"Rest. You need to conserve your strength."

Laurie's voice sounded faint, and it was as if she'd been giving herself her own advice. Trying to untie the knots had exhausted her.

"Why don't you try to sleep," he suggested.

"I'm too tired to sleep. Besides, the floor's cold."

"Just close your eyes."

Will tried to stand up. He figured if he could at least manage that, he might be able to shuffle around the garage and look for something to cut the ropes.

"What are you doing?" she asked.

"Never mind. Go to sleep."

After several attempts he finally settled on leaning his back against the slick side of the Cherokee and pushing himself upward. Once he was standing, it was difficult to move about with any speed and still keep his balance, but he used the car as support as he made his way to the front of the garage.

The muscles in his legs were cramped from the awkward position he'd been tied up in, but he was pleased that the pain in his singed leg had quieted down.

The cars in the remaining bays looked as if they hadn't been driven for a while, probably since Jacko's death—a classic Cadillac Eldorado with bullet-shaped rear lights, probably a '59, a Ford pickup, and a late-model silver Mercedes sedan, no doubt the family car.

The garage itself looked picked clean of tools, something that didn't surprise Will, given the thoroughness of the man he was dealing with. He took small steps and made his way slowly toward the Eldorado. These older cars had chrome bumpers with edges, a detail all but lost in the sameness of kidney-bean-shaped modern vehicles.

He studied the bumper of the Eldorado, rounded in front, the edges curled toward the car's oil pan. He decided that the only way he could get underneath was to lie on his belly and try to push up his roped-together hands, a position that afforded contact with the bumper but caused so much strain on his arms that he couldn't maintain any pressure.

Will rested a few moments and reconsidered, then wriggled out from underneath and, using the same technique of sliding his back up the side of the car, brought himself onto his feet again. He scanned the garage one more time.

The far corner was unlit, and he decided to investigate. As he moved closer, a door revealed itself, the outline barely visible in the shadows. He shuffled over to it, turned his back, and tested the knob. To his surprise, the door opened. He pushed his shoulder around the corner, felt for the switch, and flicked it on.

The tiny room looked as if it might have been used for storage, but the shelves that lined the walls had been emptied, save for a few cans of paint. Wickham had no doubt planned to use the garage as a makeshift lockup, and he'd cleared out anything that could have been used against him.

Will scanned the room. A barren workbench sat underneath the shelving, and, except for a 1993 calendar featuring a girl in a thong bathing suit embracing an automobile tire, the walls were empty and gray.

He was about to leave when his eye fell on a plastic garbage can underneath the bench. Maybe Wickham hadn't considered everything.

At first Will thought he might be able to lie down and kick the can out from under, but that would mean he'd have the trouble of getting up again. He turned his back to the bench and reached beneath. He could just feel the lip of the can. He grasped it and pulled. The can was heavy, but he eventually worked it out into the center of the room.

It was full of scrap wood and sawdust. Will dug down carefully. All he could come up with were a few small pieces of wood. Then he shoved the can violently with his hip, and its contents spilled to the floor.

Immediately something caught the light, a brief glint, but enough to spark his curiosity. He toed the sawdust and eventually separated from the scrap wood a round silver disk about four inches in diameter—the lid of a can.

It didn't take long for the significance of his discovery to register, but it was immediately overridden by a compelling sense of urgency. How much time did he have before Wickham came back? He had to return to the garage, close the door behind him, and work his way back to Laurie to give the impression that nothing had happened. He imagined Wickham coming back to find him gone, in fact thought he heard him when he'd tipped over the can, but it was only his mind playing tricks.

Will studied the lid peeking out from under the toe of his boot and decided the best thing was to keep it there and push it ahead as he went. He cautioned himself to take it slowly. He might have been a man trying to cross the Sahara rather than fifty paces of concrete floor.

But he managed to flick off the light with his shoulder and pull the door slowly behind him. The garage looked the same. Wickham had not returned. Will found himself silently thanking him for not having shut off the lights in the first place. Will guessed that he must look like some creature from a B movie now, sliding one foot, then the other, making slow, mechanical progress, careful always that the lid of the can remained intact beneath his boot sole.

Through the garage-door windows, Will could see the morning sunlight splashing against a stand of birch. How long had he been prowling the garage? He sensed it wouldn't be long before Wickham returned.

When Will finally reached Laurie, he found that she had managed to fight off the cold and was sleeping. He dropped to his knees. There was no graceful way to lie down, and he let his shoulder fall clumsily to the cement floor.

He lay on his stomach and rested. The floor soon pushed back hard against his ribs, and he shifted to his side and drew up his knees. The position was almost comfortable. He could feel himself drifting off to sleep and shook himself awake. He couldn't afford to waste time; he had to work at the ropes.

He fumbled for the can lid, grasped it between thumb and forefinger, but it was too awkward to control the edge. It slipped, and he cut himself. He couldn't see to check his thumb. The gash didn't feel deep, but the drops of blood on the garage floor were enough for him to pause and put pressure on the wound. It was clear he'd have to come up with a better way to use the lid. At least now he knew that the edge was sharp.

He settled on pressing the can lid against the cement floor, bending it over in the middle, and in the process fashioning a tool with two sharp edges that was much easier to maneuver. Despite his right-handedness, he found it easier, because of the way the ropes wrapped around his wrists, to use his left to saw with.

He occasionally checked his progress. It seemed to be working. The rope was fraying. It wasn't just old clothesline, though, but a high-quality, flexible nylon. What mattered was that he could cut through it. Given enough time, he'd be able to free himself.

His spirits rose at the thought, only to be dashed by Wickham's return.

————

Will didn't move. He slowly folded his hand over the bent can lid.

"I trust you both slept well," Wickham said.

Laurie jerked awake at the sound of his voice. She glanced over at Will, eyes heavy-lidded from sleep.

"Time to get rolling," Wickham said.

"Where are we going?" Will asked.

"On a little trip." He gestured toward his daughter. "You can see that Erin's ready to go."

Will studied Erin. She looked every bit the refugee, standing slump-shouldered, holding on to her backpack.

Wickham said, "We're going to take a ride in that Mercedes over there."

"Where's Candace?" Laurie demanded. "If you hurt her, I swear—"

Wickham smiled. "You don't have to worry," he said. "She's still her old hysterical self."

Will looked to Erin for corroboration of her mother's safety, but she was silent. She looked straight ahead, as if unaware of anything Wickham had said.

Wickham yanked Will to his feet. He was gentler with Laurie, a deference Will found irritating given what the man no doubt had in store for them. Wickham led them to the Mercedes, opened the rear door, and shoved Will in first, then Laurie. He slammed the door.

Wickham accomplished all this in an officious manner, like a man on a mission, and Will took it as a good sign that he was so focused. He had not bothered to check the ropes or Will's hand. He clearly didn't suspect anything, and being in the backseat meant that Will would have some time to saw at the ropes while they traveled.

Wickham opened the garage door while Erin stood watching. He lifted the trunk lid and stuffed in her backpack. He retrieved some other articles from the far bay and threw them in as well. Will couldn't make out what they were.

Wickham grabbed Erin's arm and forced her into the front

seat. He started the car after one turn of the ignition. The Mercedes purred. So much for cars that hadn't run for a while. Will thought of Robert. He probably had been the one responsible for taking good care of the Mercedes after Jacko had passed. But where was Robert now?

Wickham drove east, then veered north toward Conway. The digital clock in the Mercedes read 6:30, and the highway was busy with the morning rush. The sun was bright, the air cold, probably below freezing judging by the way people were huddled into their coats, and it felt strange being out among others, knowing that there was little chance to draw attention to the car or their situation.

The leather seats were cushy, and Will had trouble sitting forward far enough to work the sharp lid against the ropes without seeming suspicious.

Laurie was aware of his fidgeting and looked curious as to what he was up to. But Wickham didn't seem to notice. He drove, his shoulders hunched buzzardlike over the steering wheel, checking the rearview only periodically. Will sat as close to the door as possible.

On the outskirts of North Conway, Wickham turned onto the Kancamagus Highway that divides the Pemigewassett Wilderness from the Sandwich Range on its way west to Lincoln.

Wickham made good time through the twisting turns that began the route, and he hurtled along the flats, passed the sign for the Passaconaway Campground, and gunned the engine up the steep switchbacks that led to the Kancamagus Pass, the highest point on the highway.

The road was quiet except for the occasional RV or local

pickup, and Will found himself wishing for the highway congestion of foliage season. Whatever Wickham had in mind, it was clear he didn't want a lot of people around to witness it.

Will dug the edge of the lid harder into the rope, and at last he felt something give. He tried to force his hands apart, but they were still bound tightly. He wished he could see his progress, and he could only guess that he might have cut through a strand but left much of the wrap intact. Still, if he could fumble for the cut end, he might be able to loosen up the rope enough to wriggle his hands free.

Wickham turned off at the Hancock Ridge parking lot just below the far side of the pass and killed the engine. He didn't speak for a few minutes. "Looks like we've got the place to ourselves," he said finally.

Will knew the location well—to the south, the peaks of the Tripyramids, and Greeley Ponds, directly below in the valley.

Wickham turned toward Erin. "Stay in the car like a good girl," he said. He grabbed the keys, got out of the car, and opened the trunk.

"Erin," Will whispered, "don't turn around—just talk to me. Do you know what he's up to?"

"No. He didn't tell me anything."

"Listen," Laurie said, "you've got to get away from him if you can."

"How? He never lets me out of his sight."

"He's bound to make a mistake," Will said. He could hear Wickham toying with the gas cap. "Just run away the first chance you get."

Laurie said to Will, "What have you been doing with your hands?" Will explained about the can lid and his efforts to saw through. He shifted in the seat. "Can you tell if I've cut it at all?"

"It looks like there's a loose end," she said. "Hold still. Let me see if I can grab it." Her hands fumbled for his, but before she could do anything, Wickham had returned to the car.

When he found them together, he ripped open the back door and slapped Laurie hard across the face. "Get away from him!" he shouted.

Will's first instinct was to come to her defense, but there was little he could do with his hands bound. He yelled at Wickham. "Come on! You want to hit somebody, hit me!" He was conscious of his own voice, how pathetic it must have sounded, but his main concern was to draw the attention away from Laurie.

"Just stay where you are," Wickham said, jabbing his finger at Will.

"You're pretty good at beating on women," Will said. "Especially when they're tied up."

"Shut up," Wickham said. He shook his head, as if catching himself, remembering what he was about. "It doesn't matter anyway. In a few minutes nothing is going to matter."

He got in on the driver's side and cranked the ignition, tromped on the accelerator, and spun out of the parking lot. Back on the highway, he pulled over to the side and waited for a bread-delivery truck to wind its way up, gears straining, engine whining, through a series of sharp switchbacks to the top of the pass. Will had never cared for this section of road, narrow and lined with guardrails. There were just too many places to slip off, especially in bad weather. And before the road flattened out at the bottom, there was one major, brake-burning, forty-five-degree turn.

As soon as the truck passed, Wickham got out of the car. He went around to the passenger side, pulled Erin out, and told her to stand on the side of the road. Then he opened the rear door. "You two—in the front," he said. He hauled Laurie out first, then shoved Will in behind the wheel.

The car was aimed directly downhill.

Wickham walked to the front of the car and ripped open the hood. He fiddled around inside.

"What's he doing?" Laurie asked.

Before Will could answer, the engine suddenly revved.

"He's rigged the throttle," Will said.

Wickham walked to the rear of the car, and Will watched him in the rearview. He saw a white cloth stuffed into the gas tank. Part of it dangled like a tail. Then he watched as Wickham lit it. The tail burned slowly toward the mouth of the gas tank. "Shit," he said.

"What is it?" Laurie said.

Wickham ripped open the passenger door. "See you folks later," he said. Then he threw the car into drive and jumped back. The Mercedes leaped forward and careened against the guard rail at the first turn, the open driver's-side door slamming violently back a few inches inside the car.

Laurie reeled against Will, and then the force of the collision with the guardrail threw her across the seat, Will landing soon after on top of her.

"Laurie!" Will shouted. "You've got to find the loose end of this rope!"

In the moments that followed, he was conscious of their being thrown together, of Laurie's hands on his, of the rope relenting. He could feel himself grabbing the wheel, and then came an overwhelming disorientation as the windshield was blurred with images of trees and rocks, the car bouncing from side to side. He remembered hitting his head, then looking up to see the distinctive grille of a Volvo coming straight at him, reaching for the passenger door and pushing against it, his hands grabbing at Laurie, holding her as they tucked and rolled, feeling the hard pavement as they hit, the huge ball of fire that erupted, the concussive wave of sound battering his ears.

———

Will regained consciousness to the sound of a voice telling him that he was going to be all right. He opened his eyes to find an elderly man, wearing half glasses and a porkpie hat, looking back at him. For a brief moment he wondered if he'd finally met his Maker. God is *not* dead, just disguised as a retiree wearing mismatched plaids.

"Lie quiet, now," the man said. "You've had yourself a ride. "Ambulance is on its way."

Will tried to sit up. "Laurie," he said.

"Take it easy, mister," the man said. "The lady's kinda busted up, but she's still with us."

Will lay back. He was aware that he was lying on the highway, that others were gathered around him, that he'd become a curiosity. As he waited, his head began to clear. Starting with his feet, he began to test his limbs, inventorying for breakage and pain. Aside from his stinging abrasions and ripped clothing, he decided he was pretty much intact. In the distance he could hear the whoop of sirens.

He sat up.

"Please, mister," the old guy said, "don't move. They're here now."

"I'm okay. Appreciate your help." Will was gratified that

sitting up didn't produce any dizziness or disorientation. His right shoulder was stiff.

The ambulance parked just below the fire trucks near the severe S turn. He could see some medical personnel working on Laurie and someone else he supposed was the driver of the Volvo that the Mercedes had collided with.

Even though he was situated a good distance from the conflagration, he could still feel the heat. Both the Volvo and the Mercedes were engulfed in flames, and the firemen manning the single pumper looked overwhelmed with the task of fighting it. No doubt backup was on the way.

An EMT, a heavyset man with a Fu Manchu mustache, approached him and told him to lie back.

"I'm okay," Will said. "Really, I am."

"Let me check you out."

"I'd prefer you spend your time on Laurie."

"Who's Laurie?"

"The woman your partners are working on," Will said. "Now, if you want to help, how 'bout giving me a hand up?" He reached out to the man.

"You need to lie still and do what I say. You've just had an accident."

"Accident, my ass." Will felt suddenly a rush of anger, remembering how they'd ended up here. He scrambled to his feet.

The EMT tried to restrain him, but Will brushed him aside. He was fine. He was fully aware of his faculties, thank you. He headed toward Laurie. When he reached her, he found that the rescue squad had already strapped her down on a long board and were feeding oxygen through a non-rebreather mask. Her eyes were open, but she looked dazed.

"How's she doing?" Will asked the EMT who'd been working on her.

The EMT turned and squinted at Will. Her face was china-doll smooth, and she looked barely out of her teens. "Someone take a look at you yet?" she asked in response.

"Yes. She okay?"

"Well, the way she's guarding, she probably has a broken collarbone. That's all I know. You with her?"

"Yes, I—" Just as he was about to speak, Laurie made a gesture that she wanted the mask off. "She wants to talk to me," Will said.

"You can see her in the hospital."

"No. Take her mask off."

The young girl hesitated and Will brushed past her. He dropped to one knee and lifted the mask off Laurie.

"Come with me," Laurie whispered.

"You're going to be fine," he said.

"Don't go after them." She coughed once. "I know you. Don't do it."

"Okay."

"Ride in the ambulance with me."

"Sure. Just be quiet now."

The EMT with the Fu Manchu put his hand on Will's shoulder. "Come on. She needs to go to the hospital."

Will stepped back as they loaded Laurie into the ambulance. The Fu Manchu guy nodded and held the back door open. "You coming?"

"I'll catch the next shuttle."

"Then I need you to sign off first, mister." He held out a form on an aluminum clipboard.

"What am I signing?"

"That you refused medical care."

Will scratched his name in the proper space and went looking for God in the mixed plaids and a porkpie hat. He found him watching the progress of the car fire. Will tried not to think about how close he'd come to still being in the Mercedes.

"How much did you see?" he asked the man.

"What do you mean?"

"Did you notice two people at the top of the hill?"

"I saw the guy push your car, if that's what you mean. I was just coming over the pass and—"

Will stopped him by grabbing his arm. "Did you see where they went after that?"

"Yeah. They took off into the woods."

Chapter 19

"GOD" TURNED OUT TO BE JACOB BARNES. WILL FOUND out his name on his way back up the road to the spot where Wickham had sent the Mercedes on its crash course downhill.

"Tell me again exactly what you saw," Will said.

"I just come up over the pass, you know. And that fella was sending your car down." Barnes pointed to the spot on the road just ahead below the parking-lot entrance. They walked along the side of the road and passed a line of cars backed up because of the accident.

"Then what did you do?" Will asked.

"Well, I stopped, of course."

"Did that fella see you?"

"Yeah. He grabbed the girl then and headed to the parking lot."

"And into the woods?"

"Yeah. I watched him for a while before I drove over the ridge, curious about your car, you know?" Barnes stopped, placed his hands on his knees. "I need to catch my breath," he said.

"Sure." Will examined the sky. At least he had some hours of daylight working in his favor, but he knew that if Wickham had gone into the deep woods, lack of light at this time of year would soon be a problem. He reasoned that Wickham must have had a destination in mind. The man was just too careful.

Will waited for Barnes to catch his breath. A woman in a Pathfinder, queued up in traffic, rolled down her window. "You know what's going on?" she asked.

"Some kind of accident, I think," Will said.

Barnes caught up to Will and smiled wryly. "Yep, just a fender bender," he said.

Will hooked his arm in Barnes's. "You ready, Jacob?"

Barnes nodded.

Will urged him along, but he had to stop several times before reaching the parking lot. Barnes's face was red from his efforts, and Will wondered, a little too late, if he had pushed the man too hard. "You okay, Jacob?"

Barnes's chest heaved as he leaned on Will. "Just give me a minute," he said. He exhaled loudly. "Boy, it's a hike up here!"

Will looked out over the parking lot. "So you actually saw where they went into the woods?"

"Well, yeah. They disappeared over the edge of the lot." Barnes pointed to the south.

Will walked to the edge and scanned the ground. It didn't take him long to discover exactly where they had entered the woods. Their footprints led directly downhill. Wickham hadn't been too concerned with hiding their tracks, no doubt figuring that he wouldn't be followed—a point in Will's favor. But which way was he headed?

Of all the possibilities, Will decided it most likely that Wickham had a car waiting somewhere at a trailhead. As Will thought about his next move, Barnes came to his side.

"Where do you suppose they went?" Barnes asked.

Will studied his face. It had assumed a more normal coloring. "Listen, Jacob, I appreciate your help, but I've got one more job for you."

"I'm not climbing another mountain."

"This is all downhill. You'll love it."

"Best news I've heard all day."

"I want you to go back and catch up to the police. Tell

them to be on the lookout for a man and a teenage girl." Will gave Barnes an accurate description of both. "Tell them to stake out the trailheads on this side of the Kanc, especially Greeley Ponds."

"What are you going to do?"

"I'm going after them."

Barnes's eyes narrowed. "Who are they anyway?" he said. "And for that matter, who are you?"

"I'll tell you all about it later," Will said.

———

The terrain dropped steeply from the edge of the parking lot. Will dug the sides of his boots into the hill and used the branches of thickly grown fir for support as he descended into the bowl below. Wickham's and Erin's footprints, by their haphazard patterns, indicated their haste in coming off the ridge, and at one point Erin must have tumbled, for a patch of blood-stained blue denim on a broken branch indicated she'd ripped her jeans and most likely cut her leg in the process.

At the bottom the copse of fir gave way to hardwoods, mostly birch and oak, and their wider placement meant easier going. The forest canopy muted the light, and dark, heavy shadows prevented quick tracking; he had to bend down several times and trace depressions with his hand to make sure he was still on course.

He considered it an advantage that he knew the area well, and, as he suspected, Wickham was leading him in the direction of Mad River Notch, the quickest and easiest way to bushwhack through to Greeley Ponds. As he walked, he grew confident that he would eventually come upon them, but it struck him hard that he had no idea what he would do when he found them. He wasn't armed, and he was sure Wickham was. And he was dealing with a man who certainly knew where he was going, one who had experience in combat, who obviously understood how to use explosives, and who would kill him without hesitation once he discovered that he was being followed.

But surprise was an advantage, probably outweighing everything that Wickham had working against Will, if he just could figure out how best to use it.

Once he came upon the first of the Greeley Ponds, Will discovered that the footprints did not turn in the direction of the trailhead on the Kanc but led in the opposite direction, toward Waterville Valley. He stood, puzzled, then backtracked to make sure the prints were actually theirs.

Yes, there was Erin's distinctive running-shoe imprint, the worn heel of Wickham's lug sole, and they were definitely heading across the Sandwich Range toward Waterville, boldly, directly on the trail.

He should have known that Wickham would have chosen the less obvious route out. Will estimated that just a few hours of a steady pace would bring them to the trailhead where Wickham no doubt had a vehicle waiting. And here he had told Jacob Barnes to inform the police to concentrate on the trails leading from the Kanc.

The wind picked up. Will felt a chill on the back of his neck and zipped his jacket to his chin. He looked at his watch. A little after eleven. He'd been in the woods for the better part of two hours already and realized that he wasn't equipped to stay out long if the temperature dropped much further. Right now it felt below freezing, something he detected easily because his lightweight fleece jacket had lost its efficiency. He tried to imagine how much of a head start they had on him and concluded it was little more than an hour. But he knew that Erin would slow Wickham down. They would have to stop to rest, and Will was certain he could make up the time.

He set a brisk pace along the trail, not so much concerned with concentrating on every track, reasoning that Erin and Wickham had little cause to bushwhack, especially if Wickham figured that no one was pursuing. Will kept coming back to that one point: Wickham didn't know he was being followed. And if they were seen by someone else on the trail, it would be no big deal, because the news of the car wreck couldn't have traveled that fast. They would just be father and daughter out for a day hike.

He would have to be careful, though, in his zeal to catch up, that he didn't come upon them accidentally and blow his cover. The walking warmed him. Every now and again he stopped, bent on one knee, and examined their prints. He sensed he was close.

At a turn in the trail, he passed the lower of the Greeley Ponds, and through the gray, mottled sameness of the birch stand at the edge of the water, his eye caught a flash of red: Erin's jacket.

He immediately dropped to the ground and waited. He doubted that he'd been seen. He rested long enough to feel the sweat he'd generated from his hike cool against his skin and headed off trail in a crouch toward the pond.

He was directly downwind of them and had to be especially careful, but every footfall in the soft underbrush seemed amplified, and one misstep on a dried branch produced a loud snap that Will swore had given away his approach. He froze. From this vantage he could make out Wickham leaning against a large boulder. He'd apparently heard nothing. He looked engaged in a discussion with Erin. She sat at his feet, hugging her knees.

They were close to the edge of the pond, exposed on an open expanse of beach. Will had little hope of getting much closer without being detected. He considered the possibilities. He could wait for them to move and try to jump Wickham, but he wasn't sure he could take him, the former Navy SEAL who could kill a man with his bare hands, at least according to Erin's testimony. Wickham had already knocked him out once, and he wasn't eager for a return engagement.

Will decided to follow them and await his opportunity. His best chance was to somehow lure Erin away from Wickham. They were soon on the move again, and Will followed on the trail about a minute behind. He was confident now, as pursuer, that he had the advantage, but patience was the watchword.

It took another hour of hiking for them to stop again. Will checked his bearings. They were just below a junction of trails. To the left was the Flume Trail, a scenic path that led up past a gorge but dead-ended. Will had tented up there on occasion, when he felt the need to get away by himself. He was certain they wouldn't proceed in that direction.

Erin stood near the stream. She looked across it as if searching for a way out. Will moved closer. Wickham studied his map, peered at the trail sign, then folded the map and stuffed it in his jacket pocket.

Will went off trail and circled around. He figured that the sound of the water would help cover his movement and managed to get close enough for Erin to see him, if she would only look in his direction.

Wickham glanced at his watch and said something to her. He had his back to Will. She folded her arms and dropped her head.

Will took a chance and waved to get her attention, but she didn't look up. Wickham turned, and Will dropped down quickly. He could see Wickham clearly through the branches of the scrub growth, studying the very spot where Will lay crouched, hidden.

Then they were on the move again.

As Will watched them walk away, he was struck with a sense of urgency. From this point on the trail, the Livermore Road, built on the former railroad bed for the turn-of-the-century logging industry, was only about a mile away, and at the trail junction it was just a short walk into civilization. If he was going to make his move, it had to be soon.

He decided to close the gap between them. Instead of staying a minute behind, he would gauge his steps to keep them just barely in sight.

They'd been hiking only a few hundred yards when Wickham and Erin stopped and edged to the side of the trail. Will ducked off and crouched behind a thicket of birch saplings. He still had a good view of the trail, but he couldn't figure out why they had stopped.

Then he saw the dog running past them, heading up trail toward him. The dog looked to be a chocolate Lab, and behind it a woman came jogging into view. She nodded to Wickham and Erin as she passed but didn't break stride.

Will had been so focused on tracking them that coming upon someone else on the trail surprised him, but it shouldn't have. The Greeley Ponds Trail was popular for running or mountain biking thanks to its easy access, and it was used especially in the winter, because of its rolling topography, as a cross-country ski trail.

Will hesitated for a moment, then moved out of the thicket and ran back up trail. When he was certain he was out of earshot, he stopped and waited for the dog to come upon him. The dog stopped when he saw him, legs stiff, nose in the air. Will squatted and held out his hand to show the Lab he meant no harm. He hoped it wouldn't growl or bark at him.

For the moment at least, the dog merely eyed him curiously, and before it could do anything else, the woman jogged up and caught it by the collar.

"Willoughby," she said. "It's okay." She held the Lab awkwardly as she tried to jog in place.

Will approached the woman. "Listen," he said, "do you have a cell phone?" Will knew that most phones didn't work in the wilderness, but he was willing to try.

"No, why?"

"That guy you just ran by. He's kidnapped that girl."

She stopped jogging in place and stared at him. Her hair was pulled back in a jet-black ponytail, held in place by a visor with a Nike swoosh label. She was a lithe girl with an athletic build, probably in her early twenties.

"Do you know this area?" Will asked.

"Of course. I grew up here." Willoughby licked Will's leg.

"Can you cut through the woods to the Livermore Road from here without being seen?"

She looked back in the direction she had come from. "I think so."

"Good." Will started off down the trail.

"Wait a minute," she said. "Who are you?"

"It doesn't matter."

"Well, how do I know you're telling the truth?"

"Why would I make something like that up?"

She thought about that a moment. "I was really hoping to get in five miles today."

Will strode back to her and looked directly into her eyes. "Maybe you don't understand," he said. "This guy is dangerous. I'm worried for that girl's life. You need to get to a phone, call 911, and tell the cops to set up roadblocks." The flat tone of his voice had the effect of driving his point home, and the girl took one step back.

"I'll do it," she said.

He touched her arm. "I'm Will," he said. "Will Buchanan."

She nodded. "Marcy."

"Thanks, Marcy."

Will picked up the pace as he headed back down the trail, worried that he'd spent too much time with Marcy, but at least now others would know where they were located.

In his haste to catch up, he almost gave himself away when he came upon Wickham in much the same position where he'd left him. If it hadn't been for Wickham's having his back turned, Will would have been easily spotted.

Will dove off trail, and the sound of his scurrying caused Wickham to wheel around. Will froze; any movement now would certainly be a tip-off. But Wickham only stared his way for a few seconds before he turned around again. He was obviously more concerned with what was happening on the other side of the trail.

As Will watched him, he was aware that Erin was no longer part of the picture. Where had she gone?

Wickham was no doubt wondering the same thing, and that was the reason he was so focused on scanning the woods on the opposite side of the trail. Will could only imagine what had happened, but it was clear at least that Erin had gone into the woods, perhaps on the excuse to pee, and she hadn't come back yet. Wickham was savvy enough not to call out to her, because that would only serve to draw attention, but it must have been exquisite torture keeping his mouth shut. Perhaps it had been the sudden appearance of the female jogger that had reawakened Erin's resolve to resist, but Will knew that the opportunity for him to act had finally arrived. He had to get to her before Wickham did.

Wickham muttered to himself and finally headed into the woods. Will chose a route to Wickham's right. He could hear Wickham thrashing through the brush, and he sensed that the man was losing his caution, getting more and more frustrated with each step. Will could only hope that he would find her before her father did.

Then Wickham's motions became frantic, his footsteps crunching rapidly through the underbrush. Will stopped. Listened. It sounded as if Wickham had shifted from east to due south. He followed the sounds of his movement until a scream stopped him dead still. At first he thought Wickham had found Erin. Then he heard the dog barking.

Will sank to his knees with the realization of what had happened. Marcy. Wickham must have picked up the jogger's trail thinking it was Erin's. Will listened. There was no more screaming. No dog barking. He didn't know how long he had remained on his knees, but once the shock wore off, it was replaced by anger that he found difficult to control. Inadvertent as it had been, he had set Marcy up for Wickham's wrath.

Will calmed himself. As he thought it through, he realized that Wickham had just gone rushing after Erin without doing a careful job of tracking her, and perhaps she hadn't gone this far off trail at all. The most rational step was to go back to the trail and find the place where she'd entered the woods and try to pick up her tracks.

As he made his way back to the trail, he tried to block out any thoughts of Marcy. Instead he kept his focus on Erin and what was most important: that without any of his doing, she had managed to separate herself from her father, and now it was up to him to make sure he never got his hands on her again.

Will worked his way through the dense undergrowth and soon reached the spot on the trail where Wickham had been standing before his frantic chase after Erin. He could hear Wickham thrashing his way in his direction and knew he didn't have much time, but it didn't take long to find an imprint of Erin's running shoe where she'd gone into the woods. He was sure that Wickham would discover it just as quickly once he made his way back.

The forest floor, littered with leaves, made it difficult to locate prints. Will focused instead on snapped-off branches, scuff marks on rocks, and other telltale signs that led him in a soft arc back toward the trail, less than twenty yards down from where he'd entered.

He picked up Erin's prints again on the trail, and they indicated that she had crossed the path and entered the woods on the opposite side. Will muttered, "Good girl," for clearly she had, at least once since her father had kidnapped her, outsmarted him by doubling back.

And now it was only a matter of time before Will caught up to her, and he felt buoyed by the thought. Erin had found her resolve again, and it really didn't surprise him that she had it in her to fight back. This was the same girl who had run away from the rape crisis center and had stolen the money from her father for Will's bail. But, he reminded himself, she was also the vulnerable child who could be reduced, in an instant, to cowering before her father.

As he followed her trail, Will realized she had no idea where she was going. She led him on a meandering course, first due south, then sharply east, and now an abrupt shift to the southwest. He fought the urge to cry out to her, but he cautioned himself that he was still not alone, that Wickham had no doubt picked up Will's trail and was now following him.

Of that he was certain, for Wickham had gone through too much already to be foiled by a simple ruse, and Will imagined him as having recovered from his temporary fit of anger and now intensely focused again. If anything, he was even more dangerous.

Will made his way uphill, then down a knoll that led into a boulder field, and in the soil he found the imprint of Erin's running shoe. He looked ahead. The terrain flattened out, and he guessed, from his recall of the area, that he was a mile or so away from the Livermore Road, just below a group of falls called the Cascades.

There was something about the silence—it was too quiet—that suggested Erin was near. He cocked his ear to the north, but he couldn't hear anything to indicate that Wickham was close.

Will approached the area where the footprints had made clear impressions in the mud next to a large boulder. He bent down and studied the print. From behind the rock, he detected a soft whimpering.

"Erin," he whispered. "It's Will."

Slowly Erin worked her way around the boulder. When she saw him, she gasped and hugged him.

He held her. "It's okay," he said.

"I thought it was him," she said. "Oh, God! I thought you were my father."

He shushed her. "You've got to stay strong. I'm sure he isn't far behind."

She held him at arm's length. "You're alive," she said. She squeezed his arm as if she couldn't believe it. "How did you—"

"Never mind. We have to get moving."

"But where?"

"Just follow close behind."

Will studied the sun to get his bearings and then headed out on a diagonal to the southwest.

Erin struggled to keep up. "Are you sure this is right?" she asked. "Shouldn't we be going the other way?"

"Trust me."

They pushed on for the good part of a half hour, Will walking deliberately, knowing it was just a matter of time before he reached the Livermore Road.

"I need to stop a minute," she said.

"We're almost there."

"I'm sorry. I just can't go on."

"Well, drop down then. Get low." They sat hunched on the forest floor. Will listened. The woods were silent except for a squirrel nattering away on a branch above them.

"How much farther?" Erin asked.

"We're close."

"I don't believe you."

Will held up his hand. "Quiet!" he said.

She stiffened, her eyes still as stone. "What is it?" she whispered.

"Let's get going." Will grabbed her by the hand and started running. They plodded across the underbrush, branches whipping at them as they moved. The ground tilted up a slope, and through a break in the trees, Will could see the Livermore Road just ahead. He yanked on Erin's hand as he picked up speed, and she stumbled trying to keep up with him.

Close to the road, Wickham stepped out from behind a tree.

Will pulled up short and held on to Erin.

"No!" Erin screamed.

The anger and frustration in her voice resonated, and Will didn't hesitate. He charged Wickham, hoping to catch him off guard, and tackled him hard enough to smack his back against the ground. He could hear the air rushing out of him as he landed.

Will grabbed Wickham's jacket at the throat and punched his face once, hard. Wickham's nose cracked, and blood spurted on Will's jacket. He forced his hands onto Wickham's windpipe and started choking him. "Erin!" he shouted. "Run! Get out of here!"

Wickham drew a knee up and caught Will in the crotch. Will spun off him as if he'd been straddling a log and suddenly lost his balance. By the time he got to his knees, Wickham had recovered and was standing over him. "Get up," he said.

Will struggled to his feet

"Just you and me, now," Wickham said. He assumed a boxing stance and led with a quick left jab to Will's face.

"Come on," he said. "Bare knuckles. I should just shoot you, but I'm giving you a chance."

Will wasn't about to trade punches. He lunged for Wickham, and they both wrestled like two hockey players trying to get the advantage before throwing a punch. Then Wickham's leg caught Will off balance, and he pushed him to the ground.

Will quickly recovered, and from down on his knees threw an uppercut that landed below Wickham's belt. Wickham doubled over, and Will stood and followed with another right to the jaw.

None of these moves seemed to weaken Wickham. If anything, they only served to get him madder. He charged into Will, his fists pummeling Will's gut. Will tried to fend him off, but Wickham's hand speed was just too quick. Will collapsed to his knees.

Without a word Wickham stepped back and kicked Will's drooping head like he was attempting a fifty-yarder, and it snapped backward and hit a tree. The vicious blow stunned him, and as he lay there, Will was conscious enough to know that he should have felt more pain—it worried him that he didn't. He knew that his jaw hurt, but the pain was a distant throb.

He tried to get up, but his legs buckled. Wickham stuck his face next to Will's. "Don't go anywhere," he said. "I'll be back for you after I get the girl." Wickham gave Will a sharp chop to the neck, and Will fell to the ground.

He lay dazed. He never lost consciousness, but it took him some time to struggle to his feet. When he finally got up, Wickham was nowhere in sight.

Will shook his head to clear it, a bad idea. A sharp pain shot up his neck. He wriggled his tender nose and decided it was broken. His breathing was labored as he stumbled forward and followed Wickham's trail, which led him out of the woods onto the Livermore Road.

Erin should have turned right toward civilization, but her footprints clearly showed that she'd gone in the opposite direction, toward the Tripyramids. Wickham had picked up her footprints as well. Will recalled her disorientation when he met up with her in the boulder field and silently cursed himself for not explaining more clearly how to get out of the woods when he had the chance.

He pushed on, and in a few hundred yards he came to a trail junction. He turned off the road and followed their tracks past a sign that read CASCADES LOOP.

A series of waterfalls, the Cascades were a tourist favorite, especially on hot summer days, when cool dipping in mountain pools against a backdrop of cataracts provided a sublime escape. But the trail around the falls could be treacherous.

Wickham's boot prints stood out in sharp relief in a muddy area just before the trail ascended steeply past a pool to Will's left. Mist rose off the water. Will figured that the temperature was hovering around freezing, but it had not been consistently cold enough yet for the pools to ice over. The trail was slippery in places, and Will walked deliberately, mindful of his foot placement.

Then, through the sound of the rushing water, he heard Erin's faint cry. He could see her up ahead. She'd gone off trail and had maneuvered across a fallen log onto the expanse of rock in the middle of one of the steeper falls. Wickham stood on the trail talking to her, but Will couldn't make out what he was saying.

He pushed ahead. Wickham saw him coming. He reached inside his coat, pulled out his pistol, and leveled it at Will. The report was muffled, but the bullet zinged loudly by his head. Will dropped down into a gully. He was exposed on the trail and guessed that Wickham, with the thundering water as cover, wouldn't hesitate to keep shooting at him.

Wickham started across the log. Will rose out of the gully and headed up trail. By the time he got to the log, Wickham had made it across on to the expanse of rock. Erin had backed up toward the rolling water as much as she could. The water roared on both sides of them. Will looked down.

It was a huge drop, and it must have been a desperate act of courage for Erin to even think of crossing the log. It had wedged right at the crest of the falls, and the water accelerated beneath it in a deep-throated growl, tumbled furiously over the edge, and crashed to a rock-strewn pool a good fifty feet below.

Will felt helpless standing there watching as Wickham crossed over onto the rock and grabbed Erin.

Will studied the log from the land side. It had become stuck by force of water on rocks wedged into the earth. He had a passing thought that he might be able to trip Wickham up on his way back across the log by moving it somehow, but it was impossible to budge.

Wickham brought Erin to her feet. He held her by the hair and forced her back toward the log. Will headed upstream along the twisting trail out of sight. At first, he thought it best to wait until they crossed the log to follow them again, but then he spotted the deadfall, what had been a young pine about ten feet long. Part of it lay in the water. It must have been there for a while, for when he picked it up, the lower part snapped off in his hands. Will guessed that it was about three inches in diameter. He had lost about two feet of the trunk when it broke off, but it was fairly straight; the branches were sharp, ugly spines.

Will headed back down trail, holding the dead tree like a javelin. He was counting on Wickham's thinking he was still below him.

When Will arrived at the log again, Wickham had just stepped on it, his back toward Will, and he was reaching out for Erin's hand to guide her across.

Will moved faster and grasped the pine in an underhand grip. He was almost close enough to joust Wickham off the log, when Erin saw him coming.

The look of surprise on her face must have caused Wickham to shift his weight. He wheeled and teetered, reached for his gun, and, as he did, Will rushed forward and poked his chest with the tree branch. Wickham fired into the air, lost his balance, and spun into the water. The pistol flew and landed on the rock face.

If Wickham hadn't been so close to the rock, he would have immediately careened over the falls, but he thrashed the water, scrambled furiously, clawing at the sides of the rock for purchase. He worked his way crablike toward the log and grabbed it.

"Erin!" he screamed. "Help me! Help your father!"

Erin stared at him but didn't move.

"Anything!" he said. "I'll give you anything!" He reached out in a desperate effort but lost his grip. "No!" he shouted. "No!"

The water sucked him down, and his head popped up the instant he shot over the falls onto the rocks below.

Chapter 20

WILL STEPPED ONTO THE LOG AND HELD OUT HIS hand to Erin. She looked at him as if she had no idea what he wanted from her. He had to cross the log completely, and when he reached the rock, he took her into his arms. "Come on, Erin," he said. "Let's get you out of here."

"I let my father die," she said.

"He can't hurt you now."

"But I let him die," she repeated.

"We need to get on safer footing," he said. "It's too dangerous here." He managed to coax her across the log by going first, taking her hand and pulling gently. It was only when they were on the trail again that he looked down at the water.

Wickham was floating in an eddy, facedown. In his tumble over the falls, he must have landed headfirst against a rock, for above his shoulders there was nothing distinguishable except a red, pulpy mass.

"Is he dead?" Erin asked.

"I think so."

"I didn't want him dead. He was my father." She began to sob uncontrollably.

After all this man had done to her, she still felt a weird pull of blood allegiance. Will could do nothing but hold her as she leaned into him, wondering at the complex emotions she must be experiencing. He didn't say anything for a while, and eventually she calmed down. She looked up at him, her face streaked with tears. "Do you think we can go now?"

Will was more than willing to walk her out. His own

hands were freezing from the icy water, and he was sure Erin was equally cold. They headed down the Livermore Road into Waterville Valley and stopped at a local hotel. Will phoned the police and told them to send out a cop along with an ambulance. The lobby of the hotel was warm, and Erin fell asleep leaning against his shoulder as they waited on a soft, overstuffed couch.

As soon as Erin was taken care of, Will headed back into the woods with the cop, Officer Philip Templeton, to see if they could find Marcy and her dog, Willoughby. By this time there wasn't much light left, but Will felt he remembered the area well enough to find her by flashlight if necessary.

It turned out he didn't have to walk far. Just a few hundred yards up the Livermore Road, they heard a dog barking and soon discovered Marcy stumbling along, Willoughby at her heels. She described vaguely how Wickham had knocked her out with one of his vicious blows. Will commiserated, but in the darkness he was smiling. She was alive. That's all that mattered.

It was only after finding that Marcy was okay that Will began to feel tired. Templeton convinced him to go to the hospital. His shoulder was badly bruised and lacerated, but not broken. His nose was smashed, though, and he had lost a tooth. They patched him up and wanted him to stay for observation. Will refused, and they sent him home

He slept for fourteen hours by his reckoning before he was awakened by a phone call.

It was Malvina Lincoln. "Well, you've certainly been busy," she said.

"What?"

"Are you okay, Will? You don't sound so hot."

"Yeah, I'm fine. Just a little groggy. You woke me up."

"It's three in the afternoon."

"It is?"

Malvina paused. "Is anyone there taking care of you?"

"Just tell me what you want so I can get back to sleep."

"Well, I was going to give you some shit about missing the hearing and all. I mean, you've got to be one of the worst clients. . . ."

"Just tell me."

"The charges have been dropped."

"As well they should be."

"I thought you should know right away."

"Thank you. Good night."

Five hours later, when he woke up again, he could barely move. Stiff and sore, he soaked in the tub, pleased to see, with everything that had happened, that the burn on his leg didn't look infected.

As he lay there, he tried to decide whether he'd really received a phone call from Malvina. Or had it just been a dream?

———

In the week that followed, more of Wickham's exploits came to light. Because of the message Will had relayed through Jacob Barnes, police had staked out the entrance to the Greeley Ponds Trail on the Kanc, where they found Wickham's camper parked. Of the many schemes that Wickham had planned, Will thought this the most clever, for while all of law enforcement was concentrated on the trailheads on the Kanc because of where the camper had been located, Wickham had been pushing through the woods to the Waterville Valley side, where a stolen car was waiting for him. This extensive moving of vehicles explained what had taken up so much time between Wickham's visits to Valhalla, and there was no doubt in Will's mind that if he hadn't gone after Wickham and Erin, they would have made a clean break.

Laurie ended up in the regional hospital after having been treated for a broken collarbone and, in addition, kept under observation because an MRI had revealed a concussion from her tumble out of the Mercedes. After two nights she'd had enough of what she considered "pampering" and checked herself out. The driver of the Volvo had also been treated for minor injuries, road rash and a sprained ankle, and released. He apparently had seen the Mercedes careening toward him and bailed out just before the collision.

————

On the weekend Will drove his truck with Laurie to retrieve her Cherokee at the garage on the Lloyd estate. Ray had picked up the cruiser earlier in the week.

"I'm surprised Erin is with her mother already," Will said on the drive up.

"She didn't waste any time. That's all she talked about before leaving the hospital, how she needed to take care of her mother."

"A change of heart . . ."

Laurie leaned her head back and looked out the window. "I suppose if any good comes from all this . . . well, at least mother and daughter are back together."

"How's Erin doing anyway?"

"She's a strong young woman. She'll need counseling, I'm sure, but she's going to be okay."

"At least that's the impression she's giving."

"You think she's faking it?"

"I don't know, but her true reaction might be delayed. Maybe her way of dealing with all of this right now is to transfer her emotions onto her mother."

"Thank you, Dr. Buchanan."

"Okay. You're right."

"It's not going to be easy for her, I'll grant you that."

"But at least it's not your problem anymore."

Laurie looked hurt. "I never considered it a problem in the first place."

"I didn't mean it that way," he said. He drove for a while without saying anything. If *Erin* hadn't been a problem for Laurie, he didn't know what was, but he wisely didn't pursue the issue. In a few miles he said, "I just wish I knew what they talked about in the family discussion with Wickham."

She turned her head and looked at Will. "Why don't you just ask them?"

Later that afternoon Will and Laurie joined Erin and Robert in Candace's bedroom. When they walked in, Will was surprised to see Candace get up from the bed and meet them halfway into the room, Erin by her side, offering her arm for support. Candace embraced him. Will could feel her ribs through the dressing gown. She whispered "Thank you" into his ear.

Will stepped away, momentarily nonplussed by her unexpected affection. "I trust you are doing fine, Candace," he said, and immediately felt it was a dumb, awkward thing to say.

But her gaunt face lit up. "Oh, yes, I *am* doing fine. And I'm going to be doing much better, too." She turned and smiled at Erin. "Now that I have my daughter back."

"So this is a permanent arrangement?" Laurie asked. "You're going to be living here?"

Erin nodded. "For a while anyway. I need time to think things through," she said. "I'll attend the public high school. Maybe next year I'll return to Saxton Mills, but right now my place is here."

"We have so much to talk about," Candace added with a smile.

Will was struck with the change that came over her face when she smiled. She was beautiful, and for the first time he noticed the resemblance to Laurie.

Robert stepped forward then. "You'd better get back in bed now, Ms. Candace," he said. "You don't want to tire yourself."

"Don't fuss over me, Robert. I don't want to go back to bed. I'm sick of that old thing."

"Mother, please," Erin said.

"No. Let's all go downstairs into the living room. I'm sure Robert will put the kettle on."

"Yes, ma'am," Robert said.

"And I'll give you a hand, Robert," Will said.

"No need, sir."

"But I want to."

Will left with Robert and followed him to the kitchen. While they waited for the water to boil, Will said, "So where were you when all this was going on?"

"Locked in the pantry, sir. Two days."

"Did Wickham hurt you at all?"

"No, sir. It really wasn't too bad, you know. I had plenty of food. The worst was not knowing what was happening with Ms. Candace."

"You're quite fond of her, aren't you?" Will said.

Robert poured hot water into a teapot. "Yes, sir, I am."

In the living room, Will shared a sofa with Laurie. Candace sat across from them in a leather chair, a comforter around her legs, Erin on the floor in front of her. "We can't thank you enough, Mr. Buchanan," she said.

"Call me Will."

Candace nodded.

"And you don't need to thank me," he said. "I'm just glad everyone is okay." Will stood and walked toward the window. "I have to admit, though, I was concerned when Harold didn't show up back at the garage until early that morning. I didn't know what was going on."

Laurie smiled at him, knowingly, as if his segue were a little too transparent.

Candace didn't hesitate. "You want to know what happened in our 'family meeting,' as my former husband so aptly put it?"

Will turned from the window and faced her. "Only if you want to talk about it."

"Well, I didn't get a chance to say much of anything," Candace said. "He did most of the talking. He'd been in a downward spiral. He lost us, then his job—everything. He was looking to God for answers. He was a desperate man."

"In a way it was sad," Erin said. She stared at the floor. "To him it was like we'd never been apart. He thought we'd been corrupted by evil forces and that it was his job to save us. He actually thought he was doing the best for us. At one point he started crying." Erin ran her hand through her hair, and her lower lip trembled.

Laurie cleared her throat. "Perhaps we don't need to talk about this now."

"No, Aunt Laurie, I need to talk about it. I know it's going to bother me for a long time. I won't ever be able to forget it."

Candace reached down to stroke her daughter's hair. "Your aunt is right. We need to focus on the good things now."

Erin looked up at her mother. "I'll try. But it's hard."

"We both have to get better," Candace said.

————

Laurie didn't have a night off until Thursday, when she agreed to go with Will to the Burger & Brew for dinner. During the day Will found it hard to concentrate on his classes, because he couldn't stop thinking about his plan. He liked it because he thought it was romantic.

He waited until after dessert was finished and the Rémy Martin arrived before he took the package out from under his chair and placed it on the table.

"What's this?" Laurie asked.

"Present."

"Why?"

"No reason. Thought you might like it, that's all."

She stared at the package for a moment and didn't move.

"Come on, Laurie. It's not ticking." He smiled at her. The anticipation was killing him.

She took the box in both hands and shook it. Something thumped inside.

"Just open the damn thing," he said.

She untied the ribbon. "Did you wrap this yourself?"

"Of course. I watch Martha Stewart."

"No you don't."

He affected a formal tone. "You'd be amazed at the depths of depravity to which I have sunk in your absence."

"Right." Laurie finally ripped the paper. She took the lid off and separated the tissue—and pulled out one sneaker. "Oh, my God! Where did you find this?"

Will sat back in his chair, beaming.

Laurie leaned forward. "Will? Why did you wrap up my old sneaker?"

"You don't get it?"

"Get what?"

Will ran his hand through his hair. "Well, if I have to explain it to you, it destroys everything."

She placed the sneaker back in the box and cocked her head. "I guess you're going to have to help me out."

"Well, it's like, you know, you were missing one sneaker, and then I found it, and then, well, um . . . now the two shoes can be together again."

Laurie sat back in her chair and smiled at him.

"It's a gesture, okay," he said. He waved his hands stupidly.

She nodded. "And a very nice one," she said. "I'm just amazed. You thought of this all on your own?"

"Of course."

Laurie suddenly started laughing.

Will let his head drop to his chest. "Oh, great," he said. "You really know how to encourage a guy."

"No. No," she said. "It's not what you think." She stifled another laugh. "I threw away the other sneaker over a month ago."

"You did what?"

"I threw away the mate."

Will took a sip of his Rémy Martin and looked over the rim of the glass. "How could you have done that?"

"Because I gave up trying to find the other one and bought a new pair."

Will stared at the box. "I think I feel pretty stupid now."

She reached across the table and squeezed his hand. "I think it's sweet, Will."

He looked at her hand resting in his. "I hate that word," he said.

"What would you prefer?"

"Symbolic, maybe? I mean, I thought it was pretty clever, especially for me. You know, the two sneakers coming back together as we—"

"I get it, Will. You're very clever."

"Thank you."

"Now shut up and take me home."

"What?"

"You've been hogging the house for too long."